The Best of Thakazhi S. Pillai

Edited by
K.M. GEORGE

Lotus Collection 1999

This paperback edition first published in 2012

The Lotus Collection
An imprint of Roli Books Pvt. Ltd.
M-75, Greater Kailash II Market, New Delhi 110 048
Phone: ++91 (011) 4068 2000. Fax: ++91 (011) 2921 7185
E-mail: info@rolibooks.com; Website: www.rolibooks.com
Also at Bangalore, Chennai & Mumbai

Cover Design: Bonita Vaz-Shimray
Layout: Sanjeev Mathpal
Production: Shaji Sahadevan

ISBN: 978-81-7436-869-0

Typeset in ITC Galliard by Roli Books Pvt Ltd and
printed at Rakmo Press, Okhla.

The Best of Thakazhi S. Pillai

OTHER LOTUS TITLES

Ajit Bhattacharjea	*Sheikh Mohammad Abdullah: Tragic Hero of Kashmir*
Amarinder Singh	*The Last Sunset: The Rise and Fall of the Lahore Durbar*
Anil Dharker	*Icons: Men & Women Who Shaped Today's India*
Aitzaz Ahsan	*The Indus Saga: The Making of Pakistan*
Alam Srinivas & TR Vivek	*IPL: The Inside Story*
Amir Mir	*The True Face of Jehadis: Inside Pakistan's Terror Networks*
Ashok Mitra	*The Starkness of It*
Dr Humanyun Khan & G. Parthasarthy	*Diplomatic Divide*
Gyanendra Pandey & Yunus Samad	*Faultlines of Nationhood*
H.L.O. Garrett	*The Trial of Bahadur Shah Zafar*
Hindustan Times Leadership Summit	*Vision 2020: Challenges for the Next Decade*
M.J. Akbar	*India: The Siege Within*
M.J. Akbar	*The Shade of Swords*
M.J. Akbar	*Byline*
M.J. Akbar	*Blood Brothers: A Family Saga*
Maj. Gen. Ian Cardozo	*Param Vir: Our Heroes in Battle*
Maj. Gen. Ian Cardozo	*The Sinking of INS Khukri: What Happened in 1971*
Madhu Trehan	*Tehelka as Metaphor*
Mushirul Hasan	*India Partitioned. 2 Vols*
Mushirul Hasan	*John Company to the Republic*
Mushirul Hasan	*Knowledge, Power and Politics*
Nayantara Sahgal (ed.)	*Before Freedom: Nehru's Letters to His Sister*
Nilima Lambah	*A Life Across Three Continents*
Robert Hutchison	*The Raja of Harsil: The Legend of Frederick 'Pahari' Wilson*
Sharmishta Gooptu and Boria Majumdar (eds)	*Revisiting 1857: Myth, Memory, History*
Shrabani Basu	*Spy Princess: The Life of Noor Inayat Khan*
Shashi Joshi	*The Last Durbar*
Shashi Tharoor & Shaharyar M. Khan	*Shadows across the Playing Field*
Shyam Bhatia	*Goodbye Shahzadi: A Political Biography*
Thomas Weber	*Gandhi, Gandhism and the Gandhians*
Thomas Weber	*Going Native: Gandhi's Relationship with Western Women*

FORTHCOMING TITLES

Sudhir Kakar (ed)	*Indian Love Stories*
V.S. Naravane	*Best Stories from the Indian Classics*
Rudyard Kipling	*Kipling's India*

Contents

Introduction

Thakazhi Sivasankara Pillai, who is popularly referred to as 'Thakazhi', the name of his native village, is the most celebrated contemporary fictionist of Malayalam. His short novel *Chemmeen* received an international reception. The readers, however, find his short stories, which number over five hundred, equally captivating. These stories are now available in collections and anthologies. The present book contains a selection of fourteen stories which reflect his many-faceted genius.

Thakazhi was the recipient of many awards and honours, the more prestigious among them being the Bharatiya Jnanpith Award (1984), The Soviet Land Nehru Award (1974), The Sahitya Akademi Award (1957) and Vayalar Rama Varma Award (1980).

The National Sahitya Akademi and the Kerala Sahitya Akademi bestowed on him the highest honour, namely, the Fellowship. He was the recipient of honorary D.Litt. degrees of Kerala University, Calicut University and Mahatma Gandhi University. Thakazhi was recently honoured most enthusiastically by his countrymen at the time of his Satabhishekam, a customary celebration to mark the eighty-fourth birthday which coincided with one thousand appearances of the full moon. His participation was considered prestigious for any function of cultural importance in Kerala.

Sivasankara Pillai was born on 17 April 1912, in the village of Thakazhi in the Alleppey district of Kerala. His father, Sankara Kurup, and mother, Parvathy Amma, belonged to the Nayar community. Sivasankara was their only son, but he had an elder sister. Sankara Kurup was a trained actor in Kathakali, the traditional dance-drama of Kerala. His younger brother is Guru Kunchu Kurup, one of the greatest kathakali exponents of all time. Though Thakazhi's father was interested in the dance arts of Kerala, and was a competent actor, he was a farmer by profession. For him, taking part in Kathakali was only a pastime. The son inherited both these legacies to some extent as evidenced by his important literary contributions. Not only the themes, but the vocabulary and idiom used by him testify to this background.

Thakazhi has been described as the chronicler of Kuttanad, which is a waterlogged, slushy area suitable for paddy cultivation. The village of Thakazhi is a part of Kuttanad which used to be described as the rice-bowl of Kerala. It was really so till recent times, when revolutionary changes took place not only in the attitude of the people, but even in the land itself. There was very little land above water. During the rainy season all rice fields would be under water and the excess water had to be pumped out for sowing and harvesting. The floods would now and then submerge even the land where houses and temples stood. Quite a few of Thakazhi's stories can be properly understood and appreciated only if one is able to visualize this panorama. Another aspect which would aid such appreciation is the matrilineal system which was practised by the Nayars of the area till very recently.

Sivasankara Pillai's formal education was not much. In his village there was only a primary school. After completing the course there, he had to join an English school at Ambalapuzha, 5 miles away from Thakazhi. To complete the high school course he had to go to Vaikom or Karuvatta. There are two autobiographical accounts written by Thakazhi, one dealing with his childhood – *Ente Balyakala Katha* – and the other – *Ente Vakil Jeevitam* (My Life as a Pleader). In the former he admits that he was not a good student. He found the ordinary classes boring, but was interested in hearing and narrating stories. He fondly remembers a couple of teachers who encouraged his talent for storytelling, among them the well-known playwright and critic Kainikka Kumara Pillai, who was then a teacher in the N.S.S. High School at Karuvatta. An instance of his encouragement is the short story *Sadhukkal* (The Poor) published in the periodical *Service* even while Thakazhi was in school.

After completing the high school, Thakazhi did not know what to do. He frittered away nearly two years, though it was not a real waste, as he was observing and studying the life around him. Then it occurred to him to go to Trivandrum, the capital of the erstwhile Travancore State and join the Law College there to study for the pleadership examination. Life in the Law College was not as interesting as life outside in the town. His contact with the great savant and literary critic A. Balakrishna Pillai became a turning point in Thakazhi's life. Balakrishna Pillai, the editor of the periodical *Kesari*, was the presiding genius of the Trivandrum intelligentsia. Several outstanding writers and social leaders emerged from *Kesari's* coterie. Thakazhi was fortunate enough to be accepted as a disciple of Balakrishna Pillai. There he was exposed to the great writers of modern Europe like Maupassant, Chekhov, Hugo, Tolstoy, Gorky, Zola, and others. Let us read Thakazhi's assessment of the role of his guru: 'Who is Balakrishna Pillai? A power centre that stirred up the progressive thinking in all aspects of life in Kerala. The present generation perhaps does not fully grasp its significance.' (Quoted from an article in *Mangalodayam*, translated by Dr K. Ayyappa Panikkar in his book *Thakazhi Sivasankara Pillai*).

It was the Kesari Club, consisting of brilliant thinkers and writers, and the guidance of Balakrishna Pillai that gave shape to Thakazhi as a writer of fiction. And it was fiction with a purpose. Those were the days when Pragati Sahitya or the Progressive Literature Movement was influencing the whole of India. The thirties and forties of the twentieth century were particularly alive and fruitful in all the developed languages of India. Malayalam also came to the forefront and Thakazhi was in the vortex of the movement.

Inspired by the propagators of the movement and also by the great works of the West, Thakazhi launched on his career as a short-story writer. But in those days, writing was not a breadwinning career, and therefore Thakazhi's qualification as a pleader proved useful. He left Trivandrum and came back to his village and started as a vakil. Thakazhi practised as a pleader in the courts at Ambalapuzha and Alappuzha. This continued for about twenty years; but his heart was not in this profession, though it gave him a lot of opportunities to study the life and problems of ordinary people accustomed to a hand-to-mouth existence.

Fiction in Malayalam

The modern period in Malayalam literature can be divided into three phases: (i) Period of Renaissance, 1880-1930 (Neo-classicism and Romanticism), (ii) Period of Socialist Realism, 1930-1947, and (iii) The Free Age, after 1947. This is no doubt a rough division, for the evolution of literature is a continuous process and it is difficult to pin-point when a new trend has commenced.

Stories long and short have been appearing in Malayalam in a comparatively modern form since 1880. The novel and the short story came into the language as a result of our contact with English literature. Though both these forms existed side by side, the novel had precedence till about 1930 when the short story gained in popularity. The heyday of the short story in Malayalam is considered to be the period between 1930-1950. It was during this period that P. Kesave Dev, Thakazhi, Pottekkad, Ponkunnam Varkey, Basheer, Karoor Neelakanta Pillai, P.C. Kuttikrishnan (Uroob), E.M. Kovoor, Lalithambika Antharjanam and Vettoor Raman Nair established themselves as popular raconteurs. Most of these celebrities are no more with us.

The next generation of story writers beginning with M.T. Vasudevan Nair, who won the 1995 Jnanpith Award, captured the field especially after 1950. But it was Thakazhi's generation which made Malayalam literature truly democratic. It demonstrated that literature was not the monopoly of a particular caste or class who dominated the social scene. The magnificent blooming of the short story in multifarious colours made people realize that literature was not the close preserve of limited groups.

The short story in Malayalam was thus the first great medium to bring about a broad-based modern development. After enjoying considerable popularity, most of the top-ranking, short-story writers switched over to longer stories, novelettes and full-length novels. They felt that a wider canvas was necessary to paint a more comprehensive picture of life and the novel was the answer. The new novel in Malayalam thus has a history of only fifty years, whereas the old novel commences with Chandu Menon's *Indulekha* (1889) which is over a century old.

Thakazhi and his compeers gave a proletarian emphasis to their writings, especially during the Pink Decades (1930-50). Perhaps the general characteristics of their fiction could be summarized as follows: (i) Stories were more realistic and true to life; (ii) they portrayed the life of sections or groups of individuals through representative characters; (iii) the treatment was simple and direct, (iv) the motivation in general was social reconstruction. Some defects, however, should be noted to make the picture more balanced. Some writers yielded to the temptation to directly preach certain ideologies, making the muse subservient to the dictates of political parties.

Unlike others of his generation, Thakazhi lived through the next two generations and modified his stand. How did he evolve as a fictionist in the last six decades? That is a question we have to scrutinize while going through the structure and texture of his stories, especially those selected for this anthology.

Thakazhi Beyond Kerala

Thakazhi's writing medium was Malayalam, his mother tongue. He was active as a writer for sixty-five years, and his popularity was initially in his own region. Before 1940 he was acknowledged as one of the leading fictionists in his language. But with the passing of years he came to be acknowledged as an Indian novelist ranking with Prem Chand, Yaspal, Mulkraj Anand, Tarashankar and Sivarama Karanth. Thakazhi was particularly good at bringing out the forces that shape society and was adept in weaving a romantic love-episode in the social context which he portrayed. Love of a woman, lust for power and wealth move human beings in inscrutable ways and Thakazhi's fertile imagination made skilful use of these human weaknesses. These remarks apply to the vast majority of his short stories and his novels.

Thakazhi's novels

Before passing on to the short stories, let us spend a little while on his novels which number over thirty-five. The more important among them are the following:

1. *Paramarthangal* (Truths, 1939)
2. *Thottiyude Makan* (The Scavenger's Son, 1946)
3. *Thendi Vargam* (The Beggar Class, 1947)
4. *Rantitangazhi* (Two Measures, 1948)

5. *Chemmeen* (The Shrimps, 1954)
6. *Ouseppinte Makkal* (The Children of Ouseph, 1958)
7. *Enippadikal* (Rungs of the Ladder, 1964)
8. *Kayar* (The Coir, 1976)
9. *Baloonukal* (The Balloons, 1980)

Half a dozen of the above novels have been welcomed in English and in quite a few Indian languages. The Sahitya Akademi has arranged many translations. Popular publishers in English and Hindi have also found the translations of Thakazhi's novels a commercial success. The novel that has won the highest recognition outside Kerala is *Chemmeen*. This has been translated into all the major Indian languages and as many as fifteen foreign languages including English, French, Italian, German, Polish, Vietnamese, Chinese, Arabic, Singhalese, Hungarian, Dutch, Czech, and Spanish.

As far as appreciation beyond Kerala is concerned, the novel which has the second place is *Rantitangazhi* (literally 'Two Measures') and then comes *Enippadikal* (Steps of the Ladder). *Kayar* (The Coir) which some critics consider as Thakazhi's masterpiece, has not won comparable esteem in other languages and the reason is a matter for research.

It may be worthwhile at this stage to give a brief digest of the three novels mentioned above. The landless peasants of Kuttanad (his native region) have been working in the fields there for generations without adequate compensation. *Rantitangazhi* is a gripping analysis of the problems of the peasants there. The lustful life of a hard-hearted capitalist has been woven into the fabric of the story. The vigours of characterisation and the realistic portrayal of the working conditions make it a novel of absorbing interest. This novel has been largely responsible for the great spurt in Thakazhi's literary fame because of its progressive slant.

Enippadikal has an entirely different canvas. Here Thakazhi has portrayed for us the political and social life of the erstwhile State of Travancore during the period 1920-50. A young man, Kesava Pillai, who enters Government Service as a clerk, goes up step by step and reaches the very top using means foul and fair. He falls in love with a colleague, Thankamma. But being summoned urgently by his father, he goes home to learn that his marriage has been fixed. Marriage over, he returns to Trivandrum without his wife. When he comes to know that Thankamma's uncle is the Chief Secretary to the Government, he has no compunction in playing a double game. Thus he goes up the ladder and eventually becomes the Chief Secretary of the state. In the meanwhile, he brings his duly-wedded wife to Trivandrum. Thankamma becomes a sannyasini – a pseudo one at that. Kesava Pillai continues his connections with her at picnic spots. The story continues till Kesava Pillai is forced to accept premature retirement by a newly formed ministry which discovers his treacherous game.

Both these stories paint two distant social backgrounds and the interval between them as far as writing is concerned is fifteen years. And the outstanding novel *Chemmeen* emerges in between. This novel had an unusual reception in Kerala. Several editions were brought out in a matter of three years. The Sahitya Akademi Award in 1957 and V.K. Narayana Menon's English translation sponsored by UNESCO caused the novel to spread both in the national and international arenas. Its film version was also a great success, annexing the President's Gold Medal (1966). I had some indirect involvement in the attainment of this novel's unusual popularity. The first and second awards by the Sahitya Akademi were for scholarly works won by very senior writers. The third award and the first for fiction were won by Thakazhi when he was just forty-four. In those days President's awards for films were decided at the two stages, the first being the regional and the second, the national level. There was a committee for judging the films of south Indian languages and the Government of India had appointed me as the Chairman of that Committee in 1966. *Chemmeen* was ranked first unanimously and the national committee also chose this film for the President's Gold Medal. This made me particularly happy.

The story of *Chemmeen* is well known to most readers of Indian fiction and I do not have to repeat it here. It is a simple romantic story woven around a superstition which governs the attitude and activities of the fisherfolk community of the coastal regions of Kerala. Many articles have appeared in Malayalam papers praising and criticizing the novel. Some have said that *Chemmeen* is the best social novel written after Chandu Menon's *Sarada*. Others thought that the central cord of superstition was a myth. Yet others thought that since the story was essentially romantic, and did not bring in class struggle as in the case of *Thottiyude Makan* or *Rantitangazhi*, it showed Thakazhi's decline as a progressive writer. The truth, perhaps, is that Thakazhi was essentially a creative artist, and though his progressive ideas may show certain leftist leanings, no ism or creed could canalize his imaginative faculties for a set purpose. What we find in the *Thottiyude Makan* and the *Rantitangazhi* are fragments in a long social history. As a farmer, Thakazhi had realized the other side of the question he had advocated so strongly and passionately. He had written about it, but not in the form of a story. The broader and more mature view of political changes in a long span is seen in his great saga *Kayar*. *Kayar* in a way represents the culmination of Thakazhi's creative efforts to tell the stories of his people to the rest of the world. It is a long novel and a great one with many dimensions. It sketches the social history of his village and its neighbourhood, covering more than two centuries. It is not merely history but geography, economy, religion, rituals and cultural life in general. There are hardly any heroes or heroines, because the real hero is the village itself which lives, grows and transforms itself with changing times. The generations of men and women who are part of this drama are portrayed with sympathy and skill. With all its greatness it refuses to go beyond Kerala and capture the imagination of non-Malayalees, Indians and non-Indians. One major hurdle might be non-availability of adequate translations in other languages.

Dominance of the Short Story

We have already indicated the basic changes in our approach to literature during the modern period. Generally speaking, more people began to read and enjoy literature. This was made feasible by some important periodicals. In Malayalam, weeklies like the *Mathrubhumi*, *Manorama* and *Malayala Rajyam* and monthlies like *Mangalodayam*, provided good opportunities for writers with a progressive vigour and ideology. Short stories, short plays and short poems began to appear along with critical writings in these periodicals. But the most popular medium was the short story, because there you could have a good combination of narration, dialogue and description even in a short compass.

Thakazhi and his compeers really had a heyday during the Pink Decades. But in due course almost all of them switched over to novel-writing as their main avocation. Not that they gave up short-story writing. That also continued, but the focus shifted. It is in this context that we should look at the short stories of Thakazhi.

As stated earlier, Thakazhi authored over 500 short stories, and a majority of the output was before 1950. The author reported that some of them had been lost: but a good number of stories were gathered from periodicals and republished in eighteen collections. Out of these we selected fourteen stories for this collection. According to the well-known critic and poet Ayyappa Panikar, Thakazhi was an artist who matured by slow degrees (see *Thakazhi Sivasankara Pillai*, University of

Kerala, 1988). It is possible that the stories selected also indicate the stages of his growth. He remained active in the field despite the fact that new trends had established themselves, turning him into a back number. But he faced the challenge remarkably well.

The Selected Short Stories

Let us now examine briefly the selected stories and try to understand the special characteristics of Thakazhi's short stories, their thematic content and the manner of expression. Among the many collections of Thakazhi's short stories, the most important and representative one entitled *Thiranjetutha Kathakal* (Selected Stories) carries a perceptive Foreword by Joseph Mundasseri, one of the most outstanding critics of modern Malayalam literature. The collection consists of fifty-one stories. Thakazhi belonged to the small group of short-story writers in Malayalam in whom Mundasseri saw the clear influence of Maupassant and Chekhov though the situations and characters were from his own region.

As stated before, Thakazhi was the chronicler of Kuttanadu, the area around his village. The variety of life in this area is graphically presented in the stories. Thakazhi appears as the champion of the underdog. He made his stories interesting by depicting the sexual exploitation of women. Women forced to sell chastity was a frequent theme adopted by Thakazhi. Though an element of political commitment can be seen in his stories, especially in the earlier compositions, Thakazhi dealt with a variety of problems and most of his stories have a psychological slant. He had a deep knowledge of contemporary life and the situations that demanded a corrective.

The stories we have included in the selection can be grouped under four heads. Though Thakazhi Sivasankara Pillai practised as a lawyer for two decades, he was essentially a farmer. His forefathers were also farmers. His story 'The Farmer', portrays the mindscape of a traditional farmer of Kuttanad: his custom-bound, habit-ridden life, his passion for his avocation, the tenacity with which he clings to his convictions. The tragic culmination in which the picture of a person who stands up against inexorable changes being swept aside in the great march of time, yet the basic ideals and values he upholds remaining unchanged and the ultimate triumph of his compassion and generosity towards his fellow beings and nature itself – all these and more are portrayed through deft strokes. Thakazhi knew well how a naive farmer of Kuttanad would fare when faced with the unscrupulous nouveau riche, who have scant regard for ethical values. Kesava Pillai is the ideal farmer of Kuttanad.

Every year there are two or three floods in Kuttanad. The plight of the people during one of those catastrophic floods, is grippingly painted in the story 'Vellappokkathil' ('In the Flood'). In fact Thakazhi made a debut with this story. The people's desperate flight for safety and the massive loss of belongings made the natural disaster truly tragic. In such a situation people help each other. What makes the story really touching is not the expression of tender feelings of human beings, but their callous indifference to the plight of a dog. In a way, it is an animal story, but with a difference. The dog's sufferings, and its ultimate death despite its keenness to safeguard his master's property, is really touching. The story is marked by a graphic portrayal and poignant climax.

Here is another story of village life titled 'Under the Mango Tree'. It is a lyric in prose which exudes the charm of the Malayalam idiom and it was a challenge to the translator. The story is mainly about golden childhood which is lost forever. Nostalgia is too feeble a word to express the universe this story contains within its chiselled words and expressions culled from everyday life. The refrain of the children's song echoing throughout the story is like the voice of the sea heard from afar. The cyclical nature of the narration goes well with the mood of repetition – of seasons, generations, history and human destiny. Life rolls on like the waves of the ocean. This is a fascinating piece of the early Thakazhi.

The generation gap as also the conflict between the rustic village life and sophisticated city life is well illustrated in the story 'The Tahasildar's Father'. The old man, a successful farmer, has come to the end of his journey. He lost his wife sometime back and has come to live with his son who is a well-placed officer (tahsildar) enjoying all the facilities of town life. The son and his wife find his lack of sophistication intolerable. The farmer finds pleasure in singing the old customary songs of farmers during the nights. This becomes a nuisance to the daughter-in-law and to an extent, her husband. The unclean old man is not allowed to fondle his grandchild. The tension increases to such an extent that the old man decides to disappear quietly to an unknown place. In this moving story Thakazhi exposes the false sense of respectability which modern education fosters. In all such stories Thakazhi backs the true farmer of Kuttanad.

How does Thakazhi present the case of women, especially the lowly placed women of his place? Let us first take 'The Story of Kalyani'. The socialist-realist in him was against all sorts of evils bred by a capitalist society. Where the feudal landowner is all-powerful, the serfs vie with each other to get his favours. One of the resultant evils of such a social set-up would be the growth of prostitution. 'The Story of Kalyani' deals with this theme. It gives a realistic picture of the women-labourers who compete among themselves to please the landowner, and also of the go-between who gains from both parties.

Another aspect of the same problem is highlighted in 'The Story of Kettuthali'. The story centres round a widow, who, forced by circumstances, welcomes other men, to eke out a living. The symbolic significance of kettuthali (the chain or thread tied round the neck of a bride by the groom at the wedding) runs through the story like a sacred thread. Thakazhi provokes us to think about the alternatives open to the miserable widow. All through the story we are in the turbulent mind of the woman, some of whose queries might be that of the author. Her tragedy is that the men whom she trusts after her husband's death, turn out to be traitors. And she ends up a street harlot. The suggestion is that the woman who is really attached to the kettuthali has been forced to sacrifice the thread by an unfeeling society. Has she shown any disrespect to kettuthali in such a situation? The portrayal of the woman's frustration is powerful indeed.

Another aspect of the exploitation suffered by women of low castes is seen in 'The White Baby'. The misery and wretchedness of the Pulayas of Kuttanad and the degradation of their women is sharply etched in this story. The Dalits' life before their awakening is narrated with telling effect here.

What is striking, however, is the sheer inner strength and resilience that Chiruta, the female protagonist, displays in spite of her terminal condition, in spite of her sense of guilt and shame.

While we appreciate the women's point of view and their approach in such realistic circumstances, we also get a somewhat philosophic glimpse of it in the story Pativrata. This is a subtle story that redefines the conventional notion of the Pativrata ('A Faithful Wife') – a psychological tour de force that seeks to unravel some of the mysteries of a woman's heart; a family drama that reveals some of the curious twists and turns in man-woman relationships – quite different from the run-of-the-mill 'progressive' stories of the time in that it aims at a re-articulation of female desire and its repression. It raises a fundamental question. What is chastity: does it mean loyalty to the husband or the lover? A woman in our society is forced to suppress her real feelings and live an artificial life. Perhaps one can see the influence of Freud on Thakazhi in such stories.

While reading many of Thakazhi's short stories, one may wonder why he should focus on the sexual aberrations of the women folk, when the equally responsible male counterparts go scot-free. The reasons are physical and economic. The result of the unhappy union is explicitly borne by the woman for months and the social structure is such that she is always dependent on the male economically. This makes Thakazhi the champion of the dispossessed and depraved.

Is Thakazhi concerned only about life in his own area? Does he not bother about national happenings? After all, Kuttanad and Kerala State itself is a part of India. There are just a few stories which indicate his concern with national problems. Two such stories are included in the present collection.

Told against the background of the Partition, 'From Karachi' is about the communal divide that took shape on the eve of and consequent on Partition. The heroes are two street urchins named Abdullah and Krishnakumar. They become friends and jointly depend to the garbage bin behind a hotel for their food. As the news spreads that Pakistan, a kingdom for the Muslims, is about to be created, Abdullah decides to leave for Pakistan, deserting his only friend. And the parting is more painful for Krishnakumar who has never viewed his friend from a communal angle. Thus the long wait begins for Krishnakumar. In the end, a thoroughly disillusioned and sick Abdullah returns to die near the garbage bin in his friend's arms.

Thakazhi drives home the futility of making people think along communal lines, especially when the virus affects the have-nots. The street urchins deserve our sympathy; their intimate friendship, though spoilt for a while by the communal virus, is something that moves us. Though not quite outstanding, 'From Karachi' has all the main ingredients of a Thakazhi story.

'Death of Gandhiji' is a multi-layered story that raises a set of very complex questions on the role played by Gandhiji in our national awakening – the popular perception of Gandhiji as a divine spirit with miraculous powers, the attempts of the zamindars and other masters to appropriate and silence him, the catastrophic events leading to the Partition of India as well as its tragic aftermath, the communal bigotry and tensions that the nationalist movement on the whole seems not to have tackled effectively, and so on.

The narrator is one of the refugees who comes from West Punjab to East Punjab and then to Delhi. The reaction of the refugees who travel together is interesting. The old woman especially longs to have a darshan of Gandhiji at Birla Mandir. When the location is outside Kerala, Thakazhi's fiction loses its genuine vitality. But still the story has its relevance as the view of a writer from the deep south about incidents happening far away.

We have grouped some of the stories of Thakazhi though no grouping is neat and perfect. Then there are several stories which do not come under any group. Four of them included in the selection may be briefly referred to here. Though their background and social climate relate to Kerala, they could happen anywhere in India.

'The Soldier' tells the story of the loneliness of a man who has nowhere to go and nobody to love. The frenzy of the soldier to be attached to something in life is revealed in poignant terms. The irony of fate is that he relates himself to a household only to go away and die: only to find inheritors for his possessions. The inherent tragic beauty of the story makes it one of Thakazhi's best.

'An Orphan's Burial' is a short piece on the hypocrisies of middle and upper class Muslims as they encounter a wretched orphan who is denied everything in life, only to be valourized in death. A typical example of Thakazhi's work on the downtrodden and the lowest of the low, it draws effortlessly on a profound humanist spirit that sees no virtue in a mechanical or ritual observance of religious duties and rites.

They say that good fences make good neighbours. But Kerala was once a land without fences, putting to practice the abstract idea of brotherhood. Fences appeared only with the rise of petty interests in men. 'The Boundary Dispute' tells the story of two generations affected by these petty vested interests. Thakazhi disparages the attitude of the older generation that quarrels over the boundary of the land and causes bloodshed and murder. He seems to be hopeful of the people of the younger generation who take care not to repeat the mistakes of their parents, but are very rational and practical in their approach to problems.

We have already had a feel of Thakazhi's observations of the rapid social change and its impact on the culture and vision of his people in 'Tahsildar's Father'. 'The Handbag' deals with the sea-saw struggle between femininity and urbanization. Education liberated the woman of Kerala intellectually and socially, and exposed her to the possibilities of independent living and individual fulfillment. Vilasini's case is one such. She moves away from the ethics of her native culture. Her grandmother watches this alienation with distress and doubt. The story juxtaposes two generations of women that mutually disapprove of each other's ways and values. The feminists have reason to find fault with Thakazhi's patriarchal bias in the depiction of the heroine's transformation although he tried to be tolerant in his own way.

Thakazhi Sivasankara Pillai was active in the field of story writing since 1929. He brought realism to Malayalam fiction in his own way and championed the cause of the insulted and the humiliated with profound sympathy. The abused and the abandoned, the slum-dwellers, the untouchables and, above all, the poor peasants of his own native village, form the broad spectrum of human life projected through these stories. This evoked a new social awareness in Kerala. He earned a name when the literary temper of the whole of India was leftist. But Thakazhi outgrew the temptation of political commitment in the field of creative writing. His reading of Marx and Freud left a mark in his early stories, but he was never a captive of any doctrine, political or philosophical. The stories reveal that he was adept at probing the inner recesses of the human mind. He had a fantastic eye for detail as revealed from his descriptions and narrations. He evolved a simple and sharp style of prose when he essayed the psycho-analytic method of presenting the drama of human life with great sensitivity.

Thakazhi's literature has its roots in Kuttanad; but the fruits do travel far and wide, presumably because the roots are strong, going deep in his native soil.

K.M. GEORGE

In The Flood

The temple was situated on the highest spot of the locality. There, the deity stood in water reaching up to the neck. Water! Water everywhere! All the inhabitants of that place had gone in search of dry land. There was a watchman left in each of those houses which owned a boat. There were sixty-seven children in the three-roomed upper storey of the temple. There were also 356 adults, and domestic animals like dogs, cats, goats, fowl. All lived in amity. There was no discord.

Chennan-pariah (parayan in Malayalam) had been standing in water for one whole night and day. He had no boat. His master had fled for his life three days back. Even as early as when the water seeped into the house, Chennan had built a platform with coconut stems and twigs. He spent two days sitting on it, hoping that the water would recede soon. Moreover, there were four to five banana fruit bunches and a haystack. If he left the place, there would be people to snatch them away.

Now there was knee-deep water above the platform. Two rows of coconut leaves on the thatch of the roof were already under water. Chennan shouted from inside the house. Who would hear that call? Who was there nearby? There were some creatures with him whose lives depended on him – a pregnant wife, four children, a cat and a dog. He was sure that it would take only less than twelve hours for the water to flow over the roof, and that the end of his life and that of his family was drawing near. It had been raining for three days now. He somehow broke open the roof, got out and looked in all directions. There was a large boat moving to the north. Chennan-parayan hooted at the boatmen in a loud voice. Luckily, the boatmen understood the situation. They turned their boat towards the hut. Chennan pulled out the children, his wife, the dog and the cat through the opening in the frame of the roof. By then the boat had drawn near. The children were getting into the boat. 'Hey! Chennacha,' someone called from the west. Chennan turned back. 'Please come here!' That was Madiyathara Kunjeppan. He was shouting from the rooftop. Chennan caught hold of his wife and hurriedly got her into the boat. The cat also jumped into the boat. No one thought about the dog. It walked about sniffing here and there, on the western slope of the roof of the house. The boat moved away.

The dog returned to the top-most point of the roof.

Chennan's boat was already far away. It seemed to be flying away. The creature howled in death's agony. It produced a series of sounds like the cries of a helpless man. Who was there to hear them? It ran along the four slopes of the thatched roof. Sniffing certain places, it howled on.

'Dhudeem!' Frightened by this unexpected commotion a frog that had been sitting comfortably on the rooftop plopped into the water in front of the dog. The dog drew back in fear and stood there for a while staring at the movements caused in the water.

In search of food perhaps, the animal walked around sniffing here and there. The frog urinated into his nostrils and jumped into the water. The disturbed dog sneezed, again blew his nose, fiercely shaking his head and wiped his face with one of his forelegs.

The terrible torrent started again. The dog bore it sitting hunched up. Its master had already reached Ambalappuzha.

It was dark. A huge alligator floated by slowly brushing against that hut half-sunk in water. The dog barked in horror, with its tail lowered. The alligator floated by, unaware of anything.

Sitting on the rooftop, that miserable creature howled, staring into the dark and cloudy skies. The pathetic cry of that dog reached far-off places, which the merciful God of wind, Vayu, carried to the distant shores. Some of those tender-hearted men who had undertaken a vigil over the houses might have said, 'Oh! That dog is howling all alone from the rooftop!'

Its master might be having his supper on the shore. Today also, as usual, he might leave a ball of rice for the dog after his meal.

The dog howled loudly and uninterruptedly for some more time. The noise grew feeble and then died into silence. A watchman was heard chanting the Ramayana from a house in the north. The dog stood looking towards the north as though listening to it. It moaned a second time as though his throat would give way.

The melodious recital of the Ramayana flowed on once again in the perfect silence of that night. Our dog remained still for quite a long time listening to that voice till the quiet and sweet song was dissolved in the sweep of a cold breeze. There was no other sound to be heard except the roar of the wind and the beating of the waves.

Chennan's dog climbed up to the rooftop and lay there. It breathed heavily. It muttered something in despair. A fish was seen shooting up. The dog got up and barked. The frog leapt up in another part of the flooded lake. The dog whimpered in disgust.

It was morning; the dog started howling in a low heart-rending tone. The frogs stared at it. It looked dispassionately at them jumping into the water, sliding across the surface of the water and finally sinking down.

It looked hopefully at those thatched roofs which could be seen above the surface of the water. All of them were empty. There was no fire or smoke anywhere. He snapped at the flies that gluttonously bit his body and munched them. It tried to drive away the flies in his fur by scratching with his hind leg.

The sun shone for some time. It slept in that mild sun. The shadows of the banana plant swaying in the slow breeze kept moving on the rooftop. It jumped up quickly and barked at them.

The sun disappeared with the entry of the clouds. The entire place grew dark. The wind stirred the waves. The carcasses of animals floated in the water. The waves swept them away. They moved about freely, without fear. He looked at them with envy.

A small boat moved fast in the distance. The dog got up and wagged his tail and observed the direction of the boat. It disappeared into the coconut grove.

It began to drizzle. The dog looked in all directions squatting on his hindlegs, its forelegs supporting it. In its eyes was reflected the helplessness that would make anyone weep.

The rain stopped. A small boat from the northern house came forward and moored under the coconut tree. The dog wagged its tail, yawned and then howled. The boatman climbed on to the coconut tree, plucked tender coconuts and got down. He pierced the tender coconuts, standing inside the boat, and rowed away after drinking the juice.

A crow came flying from a far-off tree and fell on the rotting body of a huge buffalo. As Chennan's dog kept barking greedily, the crow pulled at the flesh and ate it nonchalantly. Satisfied, it flew away.

A green bird twittered, sitting on the leaf of a banana plant near the house. The dog was disturbed and started barking. The bird flew away.

An ant's nest that was swept by the flood reached the roof. The ants had survived, unhurt. Our dog gave it a kiss, probably taking it to be an edible thing.

Its soft snout was inflamed and reddened by continuous sneezing.

The boat moved away into the distance. The dog groaned once again. One of the boatmen turned back. 'Ayyo!'. That was not the boatman's cry. It was the dog's voice.

'Ayyo!'

That tired and heart-moving wail merged with the distant breeze. The endless sound of the waves again. No one turned back towards the dog. It remained like that till the boat disappeared from sight. Then it climbed up the roof, muttering as though it was bidding farewell to the world. Perhaps it meant to say that it would never again love a human being.

It lapped up some cold water. That pathetic creature looked at the birds which were flying above. A water-snake rushed to it playing about in the waves. The dog jumped up and climbed on to the roof. The water-snake crawled into the house through the hold through which Chennan and his family had managed to get out. The dog peeped in through that hole, edging on his feet. Suddenly alert, it began to bark. The dog availed again the voice which fully expressed its hunger and its fear for its life. A speaker of any language or even an inhabitant of Mars would understand it's meaning. It was a language comprehensible to all.

It was night. Rain started pouring heavily accompanied by a terrible storm. The rooftop was swaying amidst the beating of the waves. Twice, the dog was about to fall off the roof. A big head emerged above the surface of the water. It was an alligator. The dog began to bark in fear. The sound of fowls crying together in unison was heard from nearby.

'Where is the dog barking? Haven't the people moved from this house?' A boat loaded with hay, coconut, bunches of bananas and so on stopped near the banana tree.

The dog started barking, turning towards the boatman. It barked angrily, standing near the water with his tail lifted up. One of the boatmen climbed on to the banana tree.

'Hey, the dog is likely to jump down.'

The dog did jump forward. The man who had climbed up the banana tree fell into the water. The other fellow caught him and dragged him into the boat. By then, the dog had reached the rooftop swimming through the water, and continued to bark angrily.

The poachers cut all the banana bunches. The dog barked louder and louder as though its throat would burst. The men shouted at him, 'Hey, you will be sorry for this later.' They then carried away all the hay into the boat. The last one in the group climbed on to the rooftop. The dog promptly jumped at his feet and bit him. He got a mouthful of flesh. The man jumped into the boat, screaming aloud. The one who was standing in the boat struck the dog's belly with the punt. 'Miawo, Miawo, Miawo,' the dog's cry died down into a frail wail. The man who was bitten by the dog started crying in pain. 'Keep quiet.' The other fellow consoled him. Both of them then left the place. The dog kept barking fiercely looking in the direction in which the boat had gone for a long time.

It was about midnight. A big, dead cow came floating and remained inside the house. The dog stood at the top watching this. It did not step down. The carcass was moving slowly. It scratched and tore up the thatch, and wagged his tail. When the carcass began to move away beyond reach, the dog slowly stepped down and pulled it towards him. It then started eating the flesh with relish. There was food in abundance to meet his great hunger.

'Tup.' A resounding whack. The dog disappeared. The cow squirmed once, went down and then floated away.

Then there was no sound except the roar of the storm, the croaking of the frogs and the beating of the waves. There was no sound of the living. The kind housewatcher in the neighbourhood did not hear the helpless cries of the dog anymore. Rotting carcasses floated here and there in that vast expanse of water. The crow sat on some of them and fed itself. No sound disturbed its composure. There was no hindrance to the activities of the poachers either. There was emptiness everywhere.

After some time, the hut collapsed and sank into the water. Nothing was seen above the endless stretch of water. That faithful dog had watched its master's house till its death. It was no more. The hut too reciprocated by remaining aloft above the water till the moment the dog was snatched away by the alligator. Then it sank. It disappeared into the water.

The water began to recede. Chennan came swimming towards his hut in search of his dog. He saw the dead body of the dog lying at the foot of a coconut tree. The waves kept moving it slowly. Chennan turned the dead body over with his toe. He was not sure that it was his own dog. One ear had been bitten off. Even its colour could not be identified since the skin had rotted away.

Translated by
Jancy James

THE TAHSILDAR'S FATHER

Taitaito karkutakatattai
Karkutittai tatakataikatam.

At dead of night this loud water-wheel song was heard, a song usually heard in the months of November and December when the rice fields of Kuttanad are irrigated.

The child woke up and cried and the mother cursed it. She got up and sang a lullaby, but the child cried louder. The lullaby as well as the child's cry was drowned in the old man's song:

Taitaito karkutakatattai
Karkutittai tatakataikatam.

'Please ask him to stop that,' Bhanumati requested her husband. In her anger she beat the child. The old man was not aware of what was going on in the other room.

'Can't you please keep quiet? Why are you bawling out in the night?' tahsildar Padmanabha Pillai asked. His disturbed sleep, his wife's complaint and the child's crying – all this annoyed him considerably. The song now came to a stop abruptly.

'Hmm. What is the matter, children?'

'Can't you hear the child crying?' Padmanabha Pillai said.

'Hmm. I was just singing for joy, my son!'

Kesavassar was over seventy. His body was scruffy and wrinkled from years of work at the water-wheel and in the muddy rice-fields along with the Pulaya labourers. Rheum could be seen in the corners of his lifeless eyes and his back was hunched.

The story of his life was short: a cowherd first, a ploughman then, a tenant farmer next, he was now the tahsildar's father.

Kesavassar lived in a side room of the big bungalow. Before the arrival of the old man, the room had been used by the servants. Here he had a quilt from which the cotton peeped out here and there, a stone mortar and pestle to pound betel-nuts and a packet of betels and tobacco.

Was his life a success? Was he reaping the fruits of his sixty years of labour? Did this unlettered old man know the value of learning?

Under his bed he had no bag of gold coins. He had no vast paddy fields or groves of his own. But he had the satisfaction of having done his duty and he sang happily, forgetting himself.

Taitaito karkutakatattai
Karkutittai tatakataikatam.

When November came, he sang the song that he had learned in his youth, without realizing where he was. He had sung it for sixty years.

It was Kesavassar's son who lived in the big bungalow. When he saw clerks and even big officers come and stand before Pappan (as he called his son) with reverence and awe, and when Pappan went to the office in his official dress, his eyes would become moist. He would say, 'Ah, my Chakki does not live to see this!'

~

Padmanabha Pillai's youngest child was playing in the courtyard. The old man ran after her. Catching hold of her, he picked her up and exclaimed, 'Young wretch!' He gave her a thousand kisses and the child burst out laughing.

'Darling, call me Appooppa (Grandpa),' he said.

The child said, 'Appova'.

The old man danced for joy. The child tried to pull at his beard.

'Young scoundrel!' he said in mock anger.

Bhanumati heard this; she saw the old man kissing the child.

'Give me the child.' So saying, she grabbed her daughter from Kesavassar and went inside the house with her.

Two drops of betel-stained saliva from Kesavassar's beard had dribbled on the child's frock.

The old man overheard the mother shouting, 'Nanoo, wash the child at once! It stinks like a corpse.' And he heard the child crying too.

'Will you go again?' With this question the child received a good pinch.

Kesavassar said to the mother, 'Are you asking your daughter if she will come to me again?'

'Her frock is smeared all over with saliva.'

'Does she stink because I took her? She is my son's daughter.'

'Why do you use bad language with the children?'

'Hmm.' The old man merely grunted.

Next day the tahsildar was not at home. Kesavassar stood in his son's bedroom. The bed was smooth and glossy and the old man felt it with his hands.

The daughter-in-law came to the door and asked, 'What are you doing here?'

Kesavassar turned back and said, 'Me? You just see.' Thereupon he stretched himself on the bed.

That evening when the tahsildar returned home his wife was looking glum.

'Why make a wry face?' he asked, lifting her chin. She kept quiet.

'Oh, then I'll be angry too.' He went to his room and

changed his clothes. It was Nanoo that brought him coffee that evening.

'Bhanu!' the tahsildar called.

'What's the matter?' she asked.

'These children will get spoiled if they stay here. They are using bad language and calling each other names.'

The wife had much to say to the husband, and she told him everything.

'I've heard these names often enough myself, Bhanu!' Padmanabha Pillai remarked. 'I have received a thousand kisses from those bad-smelling lips.'

'Let me stay separately with the children,' she suggested.

'Hmm. I shall find a solution,' he observed.

Padmanabha Pillai approached the old man. He said, 'Why do you call the children bad names? They have their own names.'

The old man replied, 'Son, I don't know how to utter their names.'

'Why do you want to meddle with them? After your bath and meal, why can't you spend the time praying to God?'

The old man's face went pale. 'My son,' he said, 'When I see the children, how can I not call them and touch them ?'

Padmanabha Pillai stood motionless for a moment. It seemed to him that the dull eyes of the old man had become moist. For a moment the tahasildar's mind was full of memories – being woken up at midnight and being fed rice and curry, being hugged and kissed when he cried, being sent money while at college…

Padmanabha Pillai bowed his head and quietly went out. The old man stood there like a figure of stone.

Sometimes Kesavassar would wear just a towel round his loins and make a turban of his dhoti and go out on the road. Sometimes he would go to the court and ask the clerks, 'Is Pappan here?' At first they did not understand who this Pappan was.

'Which Pappan, old man?'

'Tahsildar – my son. The tahsildar is my son.'

Bhanumati was the daughter of a peishkar. The old man was proud of that also.

~

One day the wife of the local magistrate and the wife of the assistant commissioner (Devaswam) and a few other respectable ladies visited the tahsildar's house. While the ladies were talking, the old man entered the room. 'Hey, girl, when will Pappan come?'

There could be no greater humiliation to Bhanumati than to be addressed in this way. When all the guests had gone she was ready for a fight with the old man.

'Look here,' she said to him. 'You can't just call me "Hey girl". No one speaks to me like that.'

The father-in-law was offended. 'Then I shall call you Auntie! Phoo! Get out!'

'You can't say "phoo" and turn me out. You have no right.'

'If I don't have the right, who has? You eat my food – you bitch! I'd like to pull out your tongue, but I won't because of my son. You don't know Kesavassar!'

The old man's voice rose high. It became very loud. Hearing all the noise, Nanoo appeared on the scene.

Bhanumati wept the entire night. She told her husband all sorts of things. Padmanabha Pillai said, 'That old man is our God, Bhanu! Think about our children.'

'But I did not ill-treat him. You needn't abandon your father. He and I however cannot get on together. So I shall leave.'

~

In the early hours of the morning a noise was heard in the kitchen. Waking, Bhanumati called Nanoo. Someone had gone into the kitchen, it so seemed. She lit the lamp and went there to find out. Meanwhile Nanoo joined her.

'Who is it ?' she asked.

No one answered. Kesavassar was sitting inside. He was drinking something from a bowl. Bhanu was stunned, but Nanoo laughed.

'I got so hungry and exhausted. Did you give me my supper? I just wanted to sip something cold,' Kesavassar said, putting the bowl down.

'It would have been really awkward suppose we had struck you, thinking that some thief had broken in. What luck!' Nanoo said laughing.

Bhanumati became mad with shame, anger and fear.

'Nanoo, put all those pots outside.'

Kesavassar laughed and asked, 'With whom are you getting angry ? No, even if you give me a supper, I won't eat.'

She went to her husband and said, 'This is beneath my dignity. How can I suffer such insults? Please speak to him and straighten things out.'

'Perhaps you are not feeding the old man properly,' the husband said.

'It's always me that's in the wrong. You, both father and son, are always right. He has eaten one and a half measures of rice with just potato curry!'

'Please bear with it, Bhanu!'

A belching noise was heard from the courtyard. Bhanumati continued, 'I can't live here with such insults and scoldings – I can't.' Padmanabha Pillai kept quiet for some time; but the woman went on without a break. After some time he took the lamp and went to the side room.

Kesavassar was pounding betel-nuts. He raised his head and asked, 'Who is it?'

'Me…' the son replied.

The old man said, 'My dear son, I was feeling very thirsty and hungry. I am an old man, am I not? I went into the kitchen and drank some cold water. I thought my end had come. There was such a burning sensation inside.'

'Then, couldn't you have called Nanoo?'

'O Pappan, why should I trouble him? You know I always help myself. Now the person who would have cared for me has gone. Don't you remember, my son?'

Padmanabha Pillai who had come to chastise his father had nothing more to say. Memories, memories of childhood, choked his throat. Those emaciated hands had cooked and served many meals for him. He remembered his father's remark to an old lady: 'If I bring home another woman, she won't give anything to my son. I will therefore cook and feed him myself.'

Padmanabha Pillai went out without saying a word. His eyes were full. He walked a few paces and looked back. The old man sat crouching. He did not say a word about his supper.

Bhanumati was watching all this. She said to her husband, 'When you see the sahib, you forget the drill.'

Padmanabha Pillai did not reply for a moment.

'Bhanu, when I see that sahib, I remember the drill. There is a lot to remember. My mother!'

Padmanabha Pillai saw his dear mother, as if in a dream – his mother who had died when he was just five.

~

Father and wife – it became a big problem for the tahsildar.

The old man used to drink a little. In the evening he went out to the toddy shop. This had become a scandal. 'He goes out wearing a small towel in an improper manner and creates trouble at home,' so went the bazaar gossip.

One day Padmanabha Pillai called his father and said, 'All this is a disgrace to me.'

'My son, I shall become even more uncouth and dirty.' Kesavassar's eyes became moist. He continued, 'My lad, your father has not bowed his head before anyone. So far I have lived as I liked.'

'However that may be, this is a disgrace.'

'My... my son, do you really feel so?'

The tahsildar felt that his father's heart was bleeding. After a pause he said, 'Aunt is staying in the village.'

'Yes,' the old man nodded.

'Couldn't you stay there?'

'No, son. No.'

'I shall send you sufficient money.'

'Money! For me! I have seen a lot of money and rice in my life. I don't want money, my son. And I don't want to stay with your aunt,' so saying the old man left.

He had not undergone all the hardships of his life in order to make money. The old man did not want money. Nor did he want luxury. Padmanabha Pillai remembered his father's words in his middle age. He had said to some friends, 'When my son gets a job and is happy, I will stay with him for four days.' His whole life of struggle seemed to lead to this great desire. The tahsildar recollected scenes from his childhood. Over seventy years to be spent for those four days, and still not to be rewarded with those four days. That was indeed cruel. If only the old man had lost his memory, it wouldn't matter even if he did not have the four days. Then there wouldn't be any disappointment. But how to get on with him! The old man shouldn't be so adamant in his ways.

~

The tahsildar was out on a tour. One day Bhanumati went to the river to bathe. While she was soaping herself, her ring slipped off her finger and fell into the river. She tried her best, but could not retrieve it. When she returned after the bath, Kesavassar got to know about the incident from the eldest child. He could not stand it. He forgot himself in the loss.

While Bhanumati was changing her clothes, the old man got into the room, shouting, 'Where is the ring on your finger?'

Bhanumati did not bother to answer the question.

'Where is it?' Kesavassar shouted again.

'Hmm?' She grunted as if questioning him contemptuously.

'Hmm?' You say hmm, you have come to destroy my son. I know your extravagant ways!'

'I shall answer the person who has the authority to ask me questions.'

The old man could not put up with this insult. His veins swelled, his eyes became red. He came forward with fists clenched.

'Keep away. If you don't behave –' the daughter-in-law shouted.

Their exchange of words became heated, going beyond the limits of respectability. The neighbours gathered there.

The old man said, 'I have known your ways. My son – where is your Nanoo – that damned rascal?'

~

Next day Padmanabha Pillai arrived. Bhanumati did not rise from her bed; she had not eaten a morsel after the incident.

Padmanabha Pillai heard from Nanoo all that had happened. The old man approached the son who was bursting with rage.

'What is the use of being old? One must know what's what,' the son said.

Padmanabha Pillai gnashed his teeth.

The old man did not utter a word. Tears trickled down from his eyes.

The son continued, 'Just as in your drunkenness you drove my mother to her end!'

Kesavassar did not pay much attention. He just said, 'Son!'

The old man had much to say. His old shrunken heart had many secrets hidden in its wrinkles – not getting meals on time, Nanoo's laughter and contempt for him, and so on and so forth. He had come before his son today to speak about all this; but he was tongue-tied.

That tongue had no sweetness or suppleness, no capacity to persuade and convince.

No one had seen the deep wounds caused to that life at its fag end.

The tahsildar's bedroom was the scene of an endless conversation that night.

'That devil even said that Nanoo was another husband to me. Everyone heard it.'

When Bhanumati said this, Padmanabha Pillai jumped up.

'Did he say so?' he asked. 'Then I shall send *him* out this minute. Shameless old man!'

'Don't hurry things,' Bhanumati added. 'Please wait for four or five days, then you may do what you like.'

Thus the matter was settled for the time being.

Kesavassar had never expressed any wish to his son. The man who had never bowed his head before anyone was a mere puppet in the presence of his son. That night Kesavassar told Nanoo, 'When I see my Pappan, I am like a pussy cat. It will pain him if I say I am starving. That's why I don't tell him. You know how much my son likes me! That's why I prayed to live four days with him. All right, this is quite enough!'

~

Two or three days passed. Kesavassar did not stir out of the side room. He sat there coiled up. He looked like a madman.

'Will you come back, Uncle?' Nanoo asked. The old man kept silent.

'Master has told me to leave you *there* the day after tomorrow.'

The old man seemed to shudder. He looked back over the past sixty years. The days to come… those four days…

It was a beautiful moonlit night. The master could not get proper sleep. He woke up now and then. In his half-sleep he seemed to hear, 'Lad, call me Achcha (Father)!' Again when he was dozing off, he heard, 'Lad!' Three times he seemed to hear the word.

Next morning he woke up with endearing memories of his father. He remembered that he had not called the old man Achcha since he had passed his BA degree examination. That life – what a sacrifice it had been! Before old age crept in, that face always beamed with a smile. Is the present melancholic appearance a sign of old age?

The tahsildar called Nanoo and said, 'Call Ach... the old man.'

Just like a constable going to catch a thief, Nanoo went to the side room. The old man was not there. Nor were his clothes and betel packet. Bhanumati said that he had gone out somewhere. He was not there at noon, nor in the evening. Even the next day he was not seen. Padmanabha Pillai became anxious. He sent a messenger to his native village. The old man was not there either.

Bhanumati said, 'It's better we keep quiet. Let us say that he has gone to the native village.'

'You wretched woman!' Padmanabha Pillai fell in his chair as if struck down. 'You fiend, where is my Achcha?'

Translated by
K.M. George

UNDER THE MANGO TREE

No wind is the wind
Even a storm is not the wind
Come, O wind of Mavelikkunnam!
Come, O Sea, come
And knock down a mango for me!

Then, a gust of wind blows. In the branches of the Varikka mango tree touching the sky, mango-clusters dangle.

Their spirit rose. They yelled in unison:

Come, O wind! Come, O sea!

The wind grows in force. Something falls down, crashing through the foliage. The song stops abruptly. For a moment, there is mayhem under the mango tree. A little girl picks up what has fallen down. It is an Odollom. She throws it away, with a wry face. A little boy appears, doubling with laughter. All of them laugh uproariously. The little girl is reduced to tears.

The boy who is the author of the mischief – his name is Balakrishnan – scrambles up a nearby guava tree and takes out a mango from a palm-frond basket which is hanging from one of its branches, and hurls it before her.

The little girl hesitates for a moment to pick it up. Finally, as she bends down to take it, another boy snatches it away. Once again, there is uproarious laughter.

Gowri and Narayanan play tossing games with stones they pick up. Nani and Govindan are playing a cooking game. Neelakantan and Raman are performing the funeral rites of 'The Father mango-nut'. In a palanquin made of dry twigs, they have placed a mango-nut, and are circling the mango tree with a chant:

The Father mango-nut is dead
The ritual bath is done
Give us a mango
To complete the sixteenth day rites!

A crow caws overhead. The one who had climbed the guava tree, jumps down.

'That's a crow's nestling.'

'No, it's the mother crow herself.'

'Look! It pecks at the mango!'

'Quiet! The crow will fly away.'

Everyone is looking up.

The little girl who was made fun of – her name is Pappy – stands at a distance. The sad expression on her face has not yet faded.

Another mango falls. Balakrishnan gets it. Picking the fruit-stalk and throwing it high up to the mango boughs, he chants:

Taking this mango's sap
Give Pappy its kin mango.

Children ordinarily say, 'Give *me* its kin mango.'

But he does reparation thus, for the mischief he has already done. And Pappy gets the kin mango.

As dusk falls, the children disperse from under the mango tree. Balan and Pappy head towards their homes, hand in hand. The basket dangling from his arm is filled with mangoes. As yet she has none.

Balan and Pappy are neighbours. Her home is just next to his, on the western side.

During the next Pooja festival, both of them are initiated into reading and writing. They go together to the rural elementary school run by Kittu Asan. They return home together. They `exchange the vegetable ink, to rub on the palmyra leaves on which they write. Balan plucks lotus flowers from the temple tank and gives them to Pappy.

She is very slow in learning. She would always get Asan's beatings. She is really dumb-witted. But she repeatedly defeats Balan on one count:

The frond on that shore
The frond on this shore
The fronds clashing – what is it?

Balan doesn't know the answer to that riddle. He would say, 'coconut tree'.

'No! You lose one point!' she would laugh and clap her hands in victory.

'What is it, then?'

'The eyelids – you lose four points now.'

They would quarrel with each other. He would scratch her face. Weeping, she would make faces at him.

'I will never talk to you, Balan.'

Her family is an ancient one. So she tells him, 'We won't eat the food you people cook.'

He too has something to boast about: 'I will learn English.'

After six months of school, Pappy has to break her studies. Her uncle said: 'She won't go to school. If women are educated, they will demand accounts later.'

Next year, Balan joins a primary school. Pappy stands watching him go to school with a slate and books, and clad in a small dhoti. She asked him once: 'Balan! Does the teacher in the school spank you?'

'Yes, if I don't learn my lessons.'

In the mango season, Pappy gathers mangoes and keeps them for Balan. She gives it to him when he comes home in the evening.

She has a lot of household chores to finish. She has to tend the fire in the hearth, remove the dung from the cowshed, and wash the vessels. She practically doesn't have time even to bathe.

After finishing the course at the primary school, Balan joins the English school, 4 miles away. She looks on like a stone statue, as he goes to Ambalappuzha, clad in a new shirt, accompanied by his father.

'Won't you ever come back, Balan?' she asked.

'I will come on Fridays.'

Pappy is weeping. He is going to stay at Ambalappuzha. The little girl is dispirited. Balan comes home on Friday evening. She gives him a basketful of mangoes.

The south-west monsoon that year is terrible. There is a deluge. He doesn't come home for nearly one and a half months. Every Friday, Pappy awaits Balakrishnan's return. But he doesn't turn up.

Balan comes home, after the flood waters have drained away. There is another boy with him. He doesn't go to Pappy's house even after Saturday. She doesn't have the time to go to his house either. On Sunday, she goes to his house. Balan and his friend are learning English.

The four-year study in the middle school is over. Balan joins the high school. He comes back home only for the next Onam vacation. Pappy sees a fashionable young man going upto the house on the eastern side, a porter carrying his luggage. She goes there on the pretext of borrowing a pinch of cumin seeds. It is Balan. But, for a moment, Pappy cannot make him out.

Balan has cut off his tufted hair, he has had a proper haircut and has combed his hair attractively. His face is fair and flushed. Two or three pimples show on his face. His voice itself has changed. He is wearing chappals, has a silk umbrella. There are many interesting items in his box. There is something special about his smile.

Balan enters the kitchen saying, 'Amma, I am hungry.' Pappy is there. She is wearing only a begrimed towel reaching down to her knees.

'How are you, Pappy?' Balan asked.

She doesn't answer.

The vacation is over. It is time for Balan to go back to Alappuzha. He sets off, his trunk carried by a porter. He feels that someone called his name from under that Varikka mango tree. He turns around. Pappy is standing under the jasmin bower, in front of the Gandharva's temple. She asks: 'Are you going, Balan?'

'Hmm.'

He walks on. In Balan's heart, there are some faint stirrings. There is something undefinable in her calling out his name. It is like a disembodied voice.

Balan returns during the next mid-summer vacation. But he stays at home only for two or three days. Then he goes to North Paravur, to visit his sister.

~

Balan is in the final year at school. He has passed his fifth form that year. After a year's absence, he comes home for mid-summer vacation. Balan has turned seventeen.

That season there are plenty of mangoes, like never before. Balan who has come from the city would go and stand under that old Varikka mango tree, to get a breath of fresh air.

Children still sing that old song:

Come O wind! Come O sea!

The father mango-nut has new offspring. Pappy still runs along with the other children, as mangoes fall. Balan would watch that merry scene, at a distance. Pappy is still a child.

When she gets a mango, she pinches the foot-stalk and tossing it up, says:

Taking this mango's sap,
Give me its kin mango.

One evening, Balan is standing under the Varikka mango tree. The children have all gone home. A wind blows. Pappy appears on the scene, as if from nowhere. A mango falls. She picks it up.

'Pappy! Give me that mango.'

Pappy gives him the mango.

'You get a lot of mangoes, don't you?'

'I leave them all at your house.'

'Oh! So that's how I ate curried mango even today. Were they Pappy's mangoes?'

'I gave 150 mangoes on the day you came. Your mother told me you would come on the tenth.'

Humming a tune, he goes away. A fragrance spreads from him. The borders of the handkerchief Balan holds, are embroidered!

Pappy stands looking at Balan.

That vacation comes to a close. Balan is now a final-year student. He is studying with the aim of securing a scholarship. He does not come home either for Onam or for Christmas vacations. Balan comes home only after the public examinations.

They meet as usual at dusk under the Varikka mango tree. She bathes early, and hangs her hair loose. She wears a white, chuttip-putava (without a blouse as is the custom). For the first time, Pappy is scared while in front of Balan. A gentle breeze blows like the sigh of the Gandharva temple; a rustling sound rises in the sacred snake grove. Pappy's face is lowered. An expression of bashfulness that makes a woman's face attractive – a bright smile – plays upon her face. Balan moves two steps forward. Pappy's hands make a cross on her chest. She is eighteen.

Balan catches her hand and presses it softly. She raises her face. Their eyes meet. The next moment, Balan's grasp slackens. She disappears.

From that day onwards, she does not come to the base of the mango tree. She prevails upon her mother to have a blouse made for her. Pappy would run away and hide, whenever she would see Balan.

Balan passes the school final examination. He goes to Trivandrum, and joins the intermediate course. Thus, his world becomes wider. Fashionable friends, urban damsels – thus in that attractive life, memories of the past are buried. During that year's vacation, Balan tours the whole of southern India with some of his friends in Madras. When Balan comes for the next year's Onam vacations, there are four or five friends with him. As they go out to the fields for a walk, Balan sees Pappy standing under the Varikka mango tree; she is wearing a dotted blouse.

Four years pass. Balan becomes a graduate. He marries the daughter of a high-ranking official, now retired. The people from the locality who go to attend the marriage are all praise for the good looks of the bride.

One day, Balan and his wife come home. He is going to England, leaving his wife at home.

~

That urban girl would come and stand under the Varikka mango tree, in the evenings. Her husband has gone to that land far beyond the crimson, western sky. He had sworn several oaths at the time of parting. But, her inner self is always tossed about in anxiety. He used to say that the smiles of white ladies are very winsome, which endear them to anyone. Won't his oaths sworn to a naive girl of Trivandrum be forgotten in the course of his merry life in London? Uneducated and unsophisticated, she was never able to please her husband. She prays to God, 'Let him embrace all good things of life. And that way, let my inadequacies be compensated.'

The letters she writes to him are written with tears. 'Please don't forget the oaths you swore to me,' she would write. 'Don't be annoyed at my anxieties! I am a nitwit. I have no authority to advise you. I always pray for your success,' the urban girl from Trivandrum would go on writing. She would remember her husband petting her. His black, intertwining eyebrows, his figure, would grow in her mind. That form is her own, by rights of possession.

Standing thus engrossed in her thoughts, her eyes are filled with tears. From a distance, Pappy is looking at her with curiosity. She is in fact staring at her ornaments, and the way she dresses, covering her legs up to her feet. She is verily a goddess!

Slowly Pappy comes near her and asked: 'Why are you weeping?'

That girl from Trivandrum merely looks at her once.

~

Four years pass. Balan returns. He is appointed as a judge of the High Court.

~

That village has developed. It is fortunate enough to become the birth place of a great judge. The Thiruvalla-Alappuzha road passes that way. An English middle school, one or two coir factories – all these are there in that village.

Children still gather under that Varikka mango tree and sing those songs.

Come O wind! Come O sea...

No one knows who is the great poet who composed that song. The grandfathers and grandmothers – in their eventful youth – had forgotten those lines. But now they remember them. Even they are unable to say who the poet is.

The Gandharva temple is dilapidated now. The mangoes of the Varikka mango tree have become tiny, like gall-nuts. The children can put two mangoes at a time in their mouths.

One evening, a car stops by the roadside. A person about fifty years of age, gets down from it. His hair has turned completely grey.

It is Balakrishnan. The citizens of the locality respectfully gather together behind the honourable judge. Talking pleasantries to them, he walks to the base of the mango tree.

That old Varikka mango tree plays host by providing a mango. A mango falls right in front of him.

Some children run towards it. But, by that time, the judge has picked it up. Holding it in his hand, he looks up. Full bunches are dangling in the wind.

'Balan!'

London – noisy with the whistling of machines; his home filled with gladness by the sweet smile of his loving wife; the grave seat of justice; through his eventful life, the voice of his childhood filled with happiness falls on his ears. The judge turns around.

Body shrivelled and reduced nearly to a skeleton, a form looks at him and laughs heartily. There is not even a tooth in that mouth. The judge peers at the figure.

No wind is the wind
Even a storm is not the wind
Come O wind of Mavelikunnam!
Come, O sea, come
And knock down a mango for me!

The children sing.

Translated by
A.J. Thomas

A Faithful Wife

Husband and wife loving and trusting each other – the children grew up in such a home with vigour and enthusiasm. No one had any complaint whatsoever. At first glance, how happy and prosperous a home! Enviable, indeed!

And yet I felt that, deep down, in the inscrutable inner recesses of that home, a pot of fire stood smouldering. And every moment I expected the news that would have dire consequences. There was a grave lacuna somewhere. But no one could figure it out, just like that. A powerful and mysterious undercurrent gave their life a touch of sombre gravity. The children, poor souls, went about laughing and yelling. What was needed there was a shallow wild brook that kept pace with that peculiar rhythm. What there was, instead, was a deep river that flowed in silence!

Our mother, with her profound faith in God's mercy, would often say: 'I need not ever bother about her.' Mother too had not realized the peculiar nature of their life; whenever Mother spoke about her eldest daughter's well-being and good fortune with full gratitude, I would feel like informing her of my thoughts on the subject. But there was nothing that I could have said with a degree of certainty. A mere feeling which was quite unpleasant and which common sense would judge to be baseless and unreasonable, or else a mere shadow of a pessimist's suspicion – how, then, could it be convincingly presented? There was not a single incident or turn of expression which I could hold up as proof of my apprehension. So I did not speak a word about it to anyone. That home would break up. When? How? Why? No answer. On the whole, I felt that there was a touch of artificiality about that home. Yet I kept my thoughts to myself.

Our brother-in-law, whom we called Chettan, was the very embodiment of love. A pillar of love and strength whom we could always rely on. He helped our father repay his old debts. Not because Chechi, our sister, had asked him to, which she hadn't but because he felt that she wished it! He loved our mother like his own, for he could not help loving her as much as Chechi loved her. He got a number of gold ornaments made for Chechi and her kids. He would never transact any business without consulting her, and more, he had already gifted to her all his properties. Not that she had asked for it; one day he just went up to her and handed her the documents. Later I came to know how Chechi had stood unmoved even then, not a smile lighting up her face. Poor Chettan certainly had something coming his way!

I could never think of him without a certain sympathy. One day my mother scolded me very much for suggesting that Chettan was not really smart enough. I was sure he was in for some terrible experience. He was a mere instrument that could make possible the expression of some horrid reality. Whenever he moved over to where Chechi sat and tried to strike up a conversation, I would wonder why the poor soul should be guided by so much enthusiasm. Perhaps he was given a heart so full of love only to heighten the intensity of the tragic end of that human drama! At times he would keep gazing at Chechi and enjoying every moment of it. Why did he marry her at all?

Perhaps Chechi too had an equal degree of love and enthusiasm. Only she couldn't express it – wasn't it possible to think so?

Finally it happened – the very thing that I had imagined with a deep sense of shock. One day Chettan brought Chechi and the children to our house. The fact of their arrival was in itself meaningful. The pot of fire had exploded, and the undercurrent surfaced. The children came running in quite noisily and hugged me. Their home had broken up. I had never seen Chettan with such a grave expression on his face. Not bothering to speak to us, he left in five minutes. He did not even say a word to the children. As he walked away and covered some distance, Gomathi cried, 'Father!' and burst into tears. For he had never taken leave without hugging her and giving her a kiss.

We could not find any change of expression on Chechi's face. But it was flushed red from the experience of having encountered a moment of truth. It seemed as though she were asking herself whether it was all over.

I felt that the two of them had parted their ways after an explosion. But no one else realized it at the moment. Father asked: 'Why did Kesava Pillai go away without a word?' And Mother: 'Why – did you have a quarrel?' Gomathi came up with an explanation: 'Granny, a few days ago Father scolded her a lot. Since then Mother would often sit alone and weep. And she would look up to the sky and pray.'

Months passed. Chettan did not come back. And Chechi did not enquire about him either. Father and Mother began to get suspicious. One day Father asked her: 'Why did you have a quarrel, dear?'

No reply. The question was repeated over and over again. No answer. It seemed as if her lips were stitched up. In that silence the woman's gravity was quite a sight!

'Did you have a quarrel?'

'No.'

'Then how did this happen?'

No answer.

'Don't you want to go back to him?'

'No.'

The toughness of that answer was indeed a shock to me. Did those two letters have such power? There was indeed some deep thinking behind it. And indefinable consolation too. Poor brother-in-law! Those two letters were the reward for his enthusiasm!

'No.' Meaning she could not carry on under that yoke any longer.

She had no complaints about him. She could not say that he didn't love her. He had given her every care and attention. And there was money and property too in plenty. Such a husband would not be easy to come by. But then, how did that 'No' acquire so much power? To our parents it was a real puzzle.

Would a woman abandon her husband just like that, and that too, after the birth of four children? I wondered. Wasn't life all about compromises?

Father went to see Chettan to clear things up and was soon back. He said that Chettan was his usual self, full of affection and respect as of old. And Father had found it difficult to broach the topic during their conversation.

Chettan would not say that she was not an obedient wife. He had found her a very competent housewife as well. And their life together had not seen any disorder or waywardness. So far as her character was concerned, he would not dare to say that it was in anyway tainted. Nor was there any room for suspicion…

'No, I won't find fault with her on that score,' Chettan had said. 'No man had ever stepped into this house.' In fact the couple was a huge, indescribable problem.

Years ago, when I was a little child, I had had a certain experience of which I remembered a few vague details. At times I would try to connect those unrelated events through the use of reason. But I did not succeed in my attempts to clear away the cobwebs that obscured those scenes. It was a secret in Chechi's life, and it might lead to a solution of the current problem. But wasn't it a dream? Or was it a reality?

Chechi had moved into our house for giving birth to her last child. It was the time when Chettan was getting his house constructed. I was a little child then. Chechi stayed back in our place long after childbirth. She would often be seen walking up to the fence on the southern side and looking at someone... She was quite beautiful in those days... A warm breath fell on my body as I lay half asleep... Later an unfamiliar hand touched me... I was shocked – as if I had been scalded... Yet another night, and I heard someone say quite gently – this is how I remember that sentence: 'Would be dead in seven days.'

The next day Chettan came over to take Chechi away. She said that she would not go. Father was quite angry. At last she relented, and I too went along with them.

A few days later, Father, back home from some place, was heard speaking of someone's death. Someone who had been to our house a couple of times. I remembered him as a handsome young man with a fair complexion and a stylish moustache – the kind of person whom it was difficult to forget even after a first meeting. Somehow I felt that there was an indefinable bond between us.

In the light of such vague memories, I found myself gazing intently at my sister. Had she experienced the caressing touch of that Gandharva? Who could he be? Whoever he was, he was dead and gone, wasn't he?

But, perhaps, she could not forget him. She was a wife, and a wife had many limitations. She was indeed in full possession of herself; she could enjoy life only to the extent that it was allowed to her. Enjoying the forbidden – she would often remember the tension, the inner turmoil that it created. In the handsome young man's attempts at awakening such a woman, their vital nerves, shrunken through years of self-control, might have been aroused unawares, and it might have created an intense shock. This is how a husband is reduced to irrelevance when his wife falls for another man. Everlasting are the experiences that can awaken the feelings and emotions suppressed by discipline and self-control!

Who knows how a woman's feelings work? Once she violates a rule, she surges ahead with the desire for repeated violations. And she might trample upon whatever has been considered pure and holy till then.

I was hesitant to ask my sister about it all, though I was about to do so on many occasions. I felt that she had a lot to say, but neither of us spoke a word.

She was always lost in thought. She had something grave and heavy to think of, and she would often remain seated with her eyes turned southward. Would he come again? Perhaps that was why her eyes were brimming with tears.

Father and Mother blamed her. Father would scold her at least five times a day. He was of course right when he said that she was solely responsible for the misfortune. And he would praise Chettan. But Chechi herself never said a word against her husband, and she did not have anything to say against him. One day she seated Gomathi in her lap and said: 'Your father – '

And she went on to tell a story that illustrated how he had loved her.

After a year or so, Chettan came over to our place and demanded his properties back. And my sister agreed wholeheartedly. Chettan was astounded on hearing her reply, for it was totally unexpected. A few days later he turned up again. For no special reason. And Chechi did not speak to him. The next time he was there he put in his demand for a divorce. And Chechi agreed to it as well. Six months later the divorce was effected. And then one day we heard that Chettan had married again.

The mark of a finger print could be seen on the southern wall of the room on the southern wing of our house. I did not know who had left it there and when. One day I discovered Chechi looking at it and crying. And Chechi too later found me examining it closely. That night – it was a moonlit night – Chechi and I were taking a stroll in the courtyard when she said: 'A soul full of love lingers somewhere here, out of our sight.'

'Who is it, Chechi?'

She was choked, and did not answer that question. I saw her eyes shining with the tears brimming over.

A few days later Gomathi raised hell saying she wanted to go back to her house. And Father took her along. But she was back on the third day, crying her heart out. We were deeply disturbed and plied her with questions. She said: 'Someone… someone is staying in our house. I was afraid to go in there.'

Poor child! She went on sobbing. And she had other complaints as well: someone else was drinking gruel out of her bowl, her little toy box was missing, and so on …

None of us could console her. Let her grow up ...

Years passed. Chechi turned grey. Waiting for someone became a habitual expression in her eyes. She would also spend a lot of time meditating. What could she be praying for? Could the dead be brought back to life?

Gomathi grew up. She was big enough to understand things. One day she was seen scraping away the finger print mark on the wall with a penknife.

Chechi asked me: 'These children will hate me, won't they?'

I did not have anything to say. But I said to myself: 'Yes, they love their father. And it's just and fair.'

I felt that Chechi would tell me everything if I asked her at that moment. And she had to tell it all to unburden herself.

'Why did you make them lose such a father?' I asked.

She replied: 'I tried. Till I couldn't bear it any longer – yet I tried. It could only happen that way, dear. What does a man want a wife for? And what if she keeps thinking of someone else under his roof?'

'Who is it, Chechi?'

'The one you know, dear! Yes, the same man! As was expected, on the seventh day after I left, he died.' And she burst into tears.

After a while I asked: 'Chettan knows about this?'

'No.'

'Then why did you quarrel? You could have reconciled ...'

'I'm a chaste woman, dear, a pativrata a chaste woman devoted to her husband.'

'Pativrata?'

'Yes.'

I did not understand anything. And Chechi realized it. So she shared the ultimate secret with me.

'Since then I didn't give birth to a child.'

'But you lived there – '

Chechi said, quite mechanically: 'Lived with the father of my children.'

The whole history was thus revealed to me.

After a while Chechi said: 'I pray, I meditate, so that my god would appear at least in my dream. No, it has not happened till today. I wake up every morning from the depths of despair.'

Translated by
V.C. Harris

The Soldier

Seeing the crowd at the police station, he went in. The police officers measured the height and weight of each one and asked for their addresses. He had no answer to the question. He was one among the 150 recruited that day.

They were taken away the same day. It was an exciting journey: good food three times a day, money for private requirements and nice friends.

The train passed through many a new place. He saw many important cities. After eight days of journey, they reached their destination.

The training period was a bit tough. But it was a relief to know that one would get food – three times a day! Moreover, life was broadening, new experiences making it full of excitement. The thought that he had been a vagabond started melting away. Now he could sleep only if a bedsheet was spread out. His head needed a pillow, too. And the tongue had learned to distinguish tastes.

Life gained in scope and intensity because he felt that something could be done. He too had certain obligations, certain rights.

The regiment was taken to some place 2000 miles away. Then they were taken to another place, and after a while to a third place. By now he had learned Hindustani and had seen almost all the major cities in India. He had learned to live. He had enough money, and he was to get more from the Government.

One day an officer announced that those who wanted could go home on a month's leave, see their relatives and come back. Those who wanted leave must apply immediately. The excitement in the military camp that day could not be described. He also shared it, but the joy seemed to be lacking in something. It was no better than a fantasy.

He also put in an application.

After supper the soldiers were sitting in small groups of four or five and talking. A man from Mysore asked a man from Tirunelveli, 'Shall we start together?'

'But I want to go tomorrow evening itself.'

'I too have decided to do that. Gosh! How long it is since I saw my daughter!'

The man from Mysore sat thoughtfully for a while. His face brightened up as if he saw his daughter in his mind's eye.

The man from Tirunelveli said, 'My old mother – I ran away without even telling her. And I'm her only son.'

He too was thoughtful for a while and then said to himself, 'Poor thing! She must be waiting in the little hut for her son's arrival.'

A man whose native place was Palakkad asked Raman Nair, 'When are you leaving? Shall we go together?' Raman Nair replied quite mechanically, 'Okay'.

Another person from Madras asked in a low voice a general question seeking advice from all, 'Is there any way to extend the leave for more than thirty days?'

The man from Palakkad replied, 'You must send a telegram that you are ill. I too am thinking of doing it. I've a thousand tasks to attend to at home.' Another remarked, 'I don't think it is possible. Do you know why they sanction this leave now? To go and see our families. You must see everyone and come back. We'll be able to see our mothers and daughters again only if we are lucky. They are going to send us to the warfront.'

No one spoke. The scene suddenly became tense. The man from Mysore said with a long sigh, 'My daughter will get a thousand rupees. Oh, that's enough.'

The person from Tirunelveli said, 'Someone may nurse my mother in her last days if she has that one thousand rupees.'

The night was suffused with sighs and nobody could sleep well. Whatever they wanted to do had to be done in thirty days' time.

Raman Nair also tried to make some plans for the vacation. But nothing could be planned in detail, for he had nothing to do. The thirty days stretched lazily in front of him.

The man from Palakkad, lying next to him, asked him, 'Raman Nair, how many are there in your family?'

'No one.'

'Then where will you go during the vacation?'

He did not have a reply.

The friend asked again, 'Don't you belong to Thiruvananthapuram?'

Raman Nair felt more confused. He had no reply to that question too.

'Well, I was recruited from Thiruvananthapuram.'

'But which is your native place?'

'I'm not going anywhere. I don't want any vacation,' Raman Nair sounded very angry.

The friend asked, 'Why do you quarrel with me? Is it my fault if you ran away from home?'

Thus the talk ended.

Even during the last phase of the night one man was not asleep in the camp – Raman Nair. He wondered who had given him that name, who had added that tag, 'Nair'. No one had called him by that name in his childhood as he begged in the streets. Since when exactly in his life did this name originate?

'I'm not going anywhere. I don't want any vacation.'

The words resounded in his ears like a curse. He should not have said that so decisively. Somewhere in Kerala there might be living that unfortunate woman – his mother! Or, that man – his father! Or, someone who had come out of the same womb either before or after him. Wouldn't there be someone in the world then who might be thinking of him? Maybe he could find out.

He had seen many lands, dealt with different types of people, heard and spoken various languages. It was different in Kerala. There one did not get tired even if one went around begging. Even the water there was so special. The heat of the afternoon sun would not cause fatigue. Only the smiles of Malayalees had sincerity. Only their language could express feelings of love.

The land where he was born beckoned to him like his own mother. There came over him an ardent desire to sleep under the cool and soothing shade of coconut trees, to wander among the fields, to eat a handful of Kerala's rice.

He got up before the others in the morning. When they woke up, he was ready for the journey.

For three or four days a soldier was seen on the roads and at the junctions of Alappuzha. He used to appear several times in all parts of the city. He continued his wanderings even at night. An old Muslim porter had something to say about him to the constable on night duty at the wharf. Nobody knew where he lived or where he came from.

One day he disappeared. Next morning he was seen standing outside the closed gate of a house near Anandavalliswaram temple in Kollam. He had a tin trunk in his hand. A boy who passed by told him that no one lived there.

At that time a gentleman came out of the temple. The soldier followed him. After walking for a while, the gentleman turned towards a house.

'I'm Raman.'

Hearing the voice, the gentleman turned around. The soldier was standing there, trunk in hand, like a statue.

'Raman? Which Raman?' the gentleman asked.

The soldier stood there for a while, unable to speak. Then he walked away. The gentleman stayed there, looking at the receding figure that disappeared at the turn of the road. Raman! He could not remember anybody by that name.

The word Raman was drawn on one of the wooden boards of a hotel at Chinnakkada. The soldier told Potti, the owner of the hotel, 'I did it.'

Potti did not respond.

The soldier wandered about in Thiruvananthapuram, searching for a 'Brother Paramu'. But he was not able to locate him.

Thus seventeen days passed. He did not get a familiar smile from anyone. He moved from town to town, longing to hear the question, 'When did you arrive?' He tried hard to establish some friendship or other. The days were rolling by – five, six, seven. He attempted small talk with all the people he met, called many a person 'Brother', and smiled at everyone. But he could not retain any face in his memory, nor did any one remember him. Thus he travelled with the speed of a bird from Kozhikode to Nagercoil and spent twenty-eight days. Now only two more days were left. After each meal they stretched out their hands for money. Nobody called him by name. Why was he named at all?

~

A quiet and peaceful village, far away from the crowded cities. A small house among the greenery in the valley of a hill near the field. The soldier was having his dinner on the veranda of the house. There was a lighted lamp near him and he was restful. An old woman was serving him rice and curry from the vessels at hand, talking to him all the while.

He called her 'Amma' (Mother)! She called him 'Son' and talked to him about her family affairs.

Mother said, 'O my son, we are six! We need clothes, oil, food. Every expense has to be met. We've only a little bit of property. The year before last we got 10 quintals of tapioca from there. Shall I serve the buttermilk curry, son? After that, you can have curd.'

She served the buttermilk curry.

'You should not have served me that extra helping of rice, Amma. I've eaten too much! I must have consumed four measures of rice, isn't it so, Amma?'

'Indeed! I'd cooked only one and a half measures!'

Again the old woman resumed her talk. Raman Nair asked, 'Don't you have any son, Amma?'

The old woman heaved a long sigh and replied. 'God gave me a little boy, but took him away too. Had he lived, he would have been twenty-three now. He is younger to my Nani. Nani is two years senior to him.'

The old woman put more rice into his plate. He tried to prevent her, but she persisted.

'Let go of my hand, son.'

'It's enough, Amma. I can't even breathe.'

It was the first time that he had had a dinner like that. Nobody had told him till now that he had not eaten enough.

He strolled up and down the front yard of that small house, quite restless. It was with this godforsaken remote village that he had established an undefinable tie in his life. He felt his heart beating very peacefully. Now his thoughts became clear. He had a Mother!

Amma! Amma! 'Eat a little more rice. I'll serve you some buttermilk curry.' No, he could never forget the smile on the face of that old woman. She had wished that he should eat his fill. But suppose he had not eaten? It would not have made her miserable or rendered her night sleepless. She would not wait for him by the lighted lamp with rice and curry. For, she had not gone through the terrible agony of giving birth to him.

No, nobody would ever wait for him. Even if his body was shattered to pieces on some battlefield beyond the seas, nobody would feel the loss. No one would offer prayers to avert the tragedy.

Next morning he said to the old woman, 'Amma, may I talk to you?'

'Yes, my dear son.'

'I am a Nair.'

'You told me that yesterday.'

'I don't have any place or house to go to.'

'That also you said yesterday at dinner time.'

'Amma, I don't have anyone.' He burst into tears. The old woman stood there stunned.

A small-scale wedding took place in that house in the afternoon. Nani got a husband in her twenty-fifth year.

The evening was pleasant. The harvested field shone like gold in the glow of the setting sun. There was a mild breeze as if the field was breathing softly. A tired farmer passed him by with a plough on his shoulder, driving the oxen. The farmer attempted small talk.

'Why are you standing here?'

'Oh, nothing at all.' Raman Nair replied. Now he too had relatives.

'Why do you want to go today itself?'

He turned round on hearing the question. She was standing behind him. He looked at her intently. She lowered her face.

'I've to go. I... I... I... We'll see each other if fate wills so. Stay a virgin.'

His voice faltered.

'I will. But at least till tomorrow – '

He shook his head.

It was ten o'clock in the night and the full moon had risen in the sky. She stood watching him walk away across the field with the trunk in hand. The river went on singing its song of life.

A soldier's family allotment used to come there regularly. Forty rupees a month. She bought some vessels and cots and had her name engraved on them. The house was rebuilt with a fence around. There were plantain trees in the yard. Now she was an important figure there. Even her mother would obey her.

Every day she went to the temple and prayed. Every day she kept apart enough rice for one person. If any noise was heard at night, the mother would call out to inquire who it was.

But when her friends asked her when her husband would be back, she had no reply.

One day the postman brought a huge cover. It was the photograph of that soldier. It adorned the mud wall of the house.

Three months later, she started receiving money orders of hundred rupees every month. The amount went up after six months.

One day she got a notice asking her to collect from the police station three huge iron trunks. They contained the clothes of a top-rank military officer. In one of the boxes was the wedding garland that she had put round his neck. It was dry and withered.

Nani was startled.

After one week she received a cheque for ten thousand rupees. There were no more monthly money orders after that.

Translated by
B. Chandrika

An Orphan's Burial

And thus Makkar died. He had crawled his way to the hospital to die. During this final journey, he had been to many a bungalow on the way. Not to die there. But to get himself some gruel, a piece of cloth, or for shelter till the rains stopped. But they had shooed him away. And you can't blame them. What a bother it is to have an unclaimed corpse of an orphan in your compound!

Everyone in town knew Makkar. He had been around since he was five. And he had been begging right from that age: a handful of rice, an old rag. But as a beggar he was a miserable failure; he could never earn the sympathy of a single soul. If at all he had managed to get himself some alms, it was not because he could evoke goodness in you, but because you tended to try and rid yourselves of what was considered a pest, a stink, a hideous sight. But Makkar lived on. Yes, he lived on, unleashing an assault on you, eliciting a certain tax from you. As Habeeb Saheb, after a sumptuous lunch, retired to his first-floor bedroom and, holding his young, fourth wife close to his chest, put the seal of his love on her red lips, Makkar could be heard howling outside. What a bother! And he was not the kind who would go away empty-handed. Habeeb Saheb, resigning himself to the temporary break in his sensual pleasure, would invariably send down his wife to hand something over to Makkar and drive him away. As the familiar stink spread in the beautiful home gardens, devouring the fragrance of the flowers, the Sahebs would dig into their pockets for small change. When little kids stuffed themselves with sweet indulgences and insisted on more, the mothers would try to frighten them by saying, 'Makkar is coming!' And the kids would plug their noses and struggle to keep themselves from throwing up. And whenever anyone set out on a good job, Makkar would be the first one to be met on the way.

Makkar spent the thirty-five years of his life thus, eating cooked rice and wearing old rags. Meanwhile, there were a couple of occasions when he went about covering himself with a dirty cloth that was not stitched to size. And then he smelt of a decomposed corpse. It was heard that he had dug up a few graves in the cemetery attached to a local mosque.

All of a sudden Makkar had a bout of diarrhoea. And he collapsed. He was not even allowed to lie on the wayside, let alone at the gates of bungalows. So he crawled his way to the hospital. In the process he had lost the rag tied round his waist. It was in fact a piece of cloth earlier used as a corpse's winding sheet.

As Makkar was removed to the mortuary, the piece of cloth he had received from the hospital was filched by the scavenger. Thus, again, Makkar was completely naked.

There were four deaths at the hospital that day. Three of the corpses were taken to the cremation grounds. Only Makkar was left there. Wasn't he rotten enough? Did he have to rot further in death?

In the afternoon a few Muslim elders came in with a santuq (coffin). To take him away; to give him a decent burial. They were reluctant to give anything to Makkar when he was alive. He had to take things from them. Now that he was dead they were prepared to give him something. After all, it was good riddance!

They took him to a Muslim house nearby. Moideen, an important person in the locality, gave him a traditional bath using herbs and other perfumes. Makkar was given a fine shirt and a fresh mundu. Thus Makkar, dead, possessed a length of fine muslin cloth. Yes, it was Makkar the beggar, who lay there on the fresh soft cloth, soaked in attar and rose water!

No Qatib or priest had ever bothered about the spiritual upliftment of Makkar when he was alive. Now that he was dead, the town Qatib chanted holy verses into his ears closed for ever.

Makkar's body was taken to the graveyard beside the mosque in a decorated santuq. All the important persons in the locality took part in the funeral procession, chanting dikr and praying for the departed soul. Through the windows of the sprawling bungalows beautiful women looked out at Makkar who had found salvation from life's hardship and had merged into everlasting peace. And their ruby lips moved with the holy prayer la ilah illallah.

Thus Makkar, dead, became the public property of Islam.

The fact that there was no one to claim him when he was alive – perhaps it was because he was sullied with life. In which case, why couldn't all beggars among the Muslims strive toward liberation from that blemish? Then there would be folks to claim them. At the mosque the grave was ready. And Makkar, enshrouded in twenty-one cubits of fresh white cloth, was lowered into the grave. The piece of cloth that covered his face was removed. They turned his face in the direction of the holy land from where, 1400 years ago, the everlasting message of universal brotherhood had emanated. Perhaps the Holy Prophet whom the entire humankind must claim as their own, should be weeping, seeing how his message of brotherhood, aimed at the deepest recesses of the breathing human heart, had ended up as part of a mere funeral rite leading to the freezing cold of the grave.

As the grave was covered over with a wooden plank, Rahim Saheb, Habeeb Saheb and others threw in handfuls of earth. Yet another sign of brotherhood!

Translated by
V.C. Harris

The White Baby

It was three days since the labour pains had begun. Pathetic cries emerged from the isolation hut. She was in great pain.

Karkataka – the month of the rains... Floods... The sun hidden from sight for a week... The wind raging... In the middle of a big paddy field inundated by the mounting waves stood the lowly homestead of the untouchable Parayas. No other houses nearby. The neighbourhood was a distant stretch of land, frozen in the wind and the cold, and obscured from view by the rain.

The wails of her agony rose amidst the howling storm. Ittiathi started, and rose to his feet. Then he stepped out and hurried towards the isolation hut.

She cried out in agony: 'Oh damn him! Damn the bloody sinner! I can't take it any longer!'

Who could be the sinner?

Ittiathi was pained by an unidentifiable guilt. He called out to her: 'How should I know?'

Chiruta was cursing the man who was responsible for her plight. He was the sinner. And Ittiathi knew it. So he decided: 'No more of this!'

Ittiathi heard some sound emerging from the isolation hut, and he asked with great anxiety: 'How's it going?'

'Go away!' said the woman.

Ittiathi longed to go in and beg her to forgive him for his sins, to assure her that what had happened would never be repeated.

It was the end of a sequence of dreams dear to his heart, and a turning point in his life. When your wife, with a sweet shyness, tells you about the new life in her womb, how delighted you feel!

Ittiathi would often gently stroke her stomach and watch the growth of the body. How many times had he kissed the hidden treasure with pride! Oh, to see the dark, chubby baby-boy! Ten years... sixteen years... he grows up... and then there won't be any need to waste good money on renting outside help at farming. The boy would grow up to be a young stout Ittiathi by then!

Dark and lovely skin, curly hair, large eyes, a healthy physique – she was quite a beauty among the Parayas. She would always wear a white mundu and keep her hair combed and tidy. She would have a bath every day and put on bindi. The older Paraya women used to call her a flirt. And she looked one.

The evening was barely getting over and yet it was pitch dark. The wind and the rain had not subsided, and the water kept rising.

Neeli, the Paraya midwife, came out of the hut and told Ittiathi that the whole thing was beyond her.

'Go, get the woman from Kannanthra,' she said.

For a moment Ittiathi was lost in thought. How was he to bring the old nurse without a boat? Then, tying up the sparse cotton towel round his head, he dived into the rainy waters. Only the howling of the wind and the sound of the waves could be heard. And on the other bank a row of lights shone like stars.

A little kerosene lamp was burning in the hut. As the thatched roof was blown off by the wind and the rain, the lamp began to flicker and fail. The pregnant woman was lying on a tattered mat. Water began to seep in.

Agonising wails. And she kept cursing and swearing. Neeli said, her eyes welling up with tears, 'Don't swear, my girl.' And she said the Almighty would protect her.

'I'll die,' Chiruta answered. 'I want to die. Only die!' Despite the chilling cold, Chiruta was sweating profusely.

She couldn't sit up, couldn't lie down, couldn't get up. Even the seasoned midwife felt sorry for the poor girl. 'Perhaps she will die. If only this world could be rid of such labour, such pain!'

Neeli was anxiously looking out for Ittiathi. All the lights on the other bank had been put out. Neeli peered into the darkness. 'Where is he?'

'Gone to fetch the Kannanthra woman.'

'Why bother him?'

'Who else is there, my child, to do all this?'

Chiruta went on cursing some great sinner.

For a while Chiruta was lost in thought. Then she said to Neeli, 'Ammachi, please sing that Naachi song for me... So that I may doze off.'

Neeli obliged.

'*Tharana tharana tharana thaiyyom...*'

The screeching winds crippled the unrefined music which spread all over the little hut. Some unknown ancient Paraya poet, the cultural representative of the community, had composed those lines, unmindful of the purity or perfection of word or song.

There was a story which was very popular among the members of the Paraya community who knew no refinement. The ancient story of a young Paraya woman who was defiled and who was punished for her fall. And the song was all about that story. It was a story that every Paraya girl learned from her mother or at the workplace. The legend of the girl from olden times – there was only one Paraya girl in their history who had gone astray.

While Neeli sang, Chiruta said, 'Ammachi, I shall tell you something. Please don't tell anyone else.'

'No, my little child.'

'Nothing, it's nothing.'

Chiruta decided not to speak, and Neeli didn't force her.

Oroatha, the Kannanthra woman, came in, lifting the mat

that served as a door to the hut. The draught that stole into the gloomy hut blew out the kerosene lamp. And there was no fire to light it again.

Ittiathi once again disappeared into the vast night in the little boat that he had borrowed from someone to fetch Oroatha.

Neeli was talking to Oroatha. And Chiruta was screaming all the while. Oroatha chided her: 'All this is but a woman's lot, girl!'

'I don't want it! I want only to die!'

'Die! What a time for jokes! God willing, we can finish this job in a couple of hours.'

'No! No!'

Chiruta went on cursing, and Neeli advised her against it. 'Her man… meek and docile as the cow – except that he eats no grass! She is his very life, and see how much trouble he takes.'

'Ammachi, it's not him!'

Oroatha was getting impatient. 'Who else then? The Almighty?'

Chiruta kept on asking about the fallen Paraya woman. How was she spoiled? The song didn't make it clear. Neeli offered to sing it once more. But Chiruta couldn't bear to hear it. Was that girl pregnant from her folly? Did she give birth to a baby? Did he grow up as a good soul, or did he go astray?

'Why should you know about all that?'

'Just to know… Ammachi, I want to tell you something. Don't tell anyone else.'

'No, my girl.'

'When the bungalow was being built, I went there for work…' Neeli was listening, but Chiruta didn't continue.

Ittiathi came back with a stick of fire. That he had managed to keep the fire alive in the rain was a marvel.

Oroatha examined Chiruta and ordered for some oil. There was no oil in the hut. Oroatha chided Ittiathi and said he should have known his duties.

Chiruta asked, 'Why should he?'

Ittiathi was shocked. Oroatha's harsh words had in fact consoled him. But now Chiruta was asking them why he should know anything. Was she blaming him, or expressing her dissatisfaction? Did he deny her anything? No.

'Chiruta, how would I now about the oil?'

'That's not what I meant.'

More screams! 'Hold down the arms to the ground!' What torture, what atrocities were going on inside? She was screaming with pain. Ittiathi was almost insane with fear and anxiety. He sought after every god he knew in his hour of need.

The raging storm and the rising waves shook the flimsy little hut. Not a soul took pity on the agonies and anxieties of the poor souls in that hut. Not a light blinked anywhere in sight. Far away on the other bank, the master's bungalows were tucked away in a blanket of darkness, and the same blanket held within its folds a little hut too with all its secret sorrows.

For a while Ittiathi could not hear Chiruta's voice; he could hear only the other two women whispering. And his heart was about to burst. He called out to Oroatha. No one responded. Ittiathi peeped into the hut through the gaps on the palm-leaf wall. Chiruta was stretched out on the mat, bathed in blood, her belly still large and bulging.

'Oh, my dear Chirutha!' Ittiathi's loud groan brought Neeli out of the hut. She took him back to the main hut.

The lamp went out. And Neeli began to wail again. Ittiathi went out again in the boat to buy some kerosene.

After a while Chiruta asked Neeli, 'Ammachi, is it true?'

'What, my little child?'

'The song.'

'Yes, dear. Should I sing it for you?'

'No, Ammachi. I don't want to hear it!'

In the darkness she lifted her arms to embrace someone. Someone was there, smiling at her. She felt someone's tears falling on her face.

'Ammachi, I shouldn't have worn a fresh white mundu. I shouldn't have kept my hair combed. I should've gone about dirty and stinking.'

'Why, dear?'

'It is so!' And she gave three or four blows on her belly. Neeli grabbed her hand and stopped her.

'Let it die, Ammachi!'

'He's waiting for the little baby.'

'Why should he wait for this one?'

'Why not, my dear?'

'Ammachi, when the bungalow was being built, I went there for work.'

'So?'

'Nothing.'

A great agony was burning away her soul and that was more tormenting to her than her labour. Neeli couldn't see that. Chiruta asked again, 'Ammachi, that fallen Paraya woman – did she wear a white cloth? Was she given a gold coin – ?'

Neeli was baffled.

Ittiathi came in dripping wet and shivering all over. On his way back with kerosene the little boat had capsized.

At the break of dawn the rain stopped. But the wind raged on. Another inch of water, and the hut would be flooded.

Chiruta's belly had grown as large as a hutment. She lay motionless on her back. And she continued to curse and swear.

Now she said to Neeli, 'Sinners will be punished by the Almighty, won't they, Ammachi?'

'But what did you do, daughter?'

'Oh, Ammachi… has only one woman been spoiled so far?'

'Yes, dear.'

'But… I'm spoiled too!'

Neeli was stunned. Her arms that held Chiruta tightly withdrew all of a sudden, as if scalded.

'Ammachi, don't touch me. You too will be tainted!'

The Paraya women of Kuttanad had great wealth – the kind of wealth which even their feudal mistresses could not boast of. Only one among them had so far been spoiled.

'Ammachi, please sing that song for me.'

Neeli remained silent.

'Ammachi, are you angry with me?'

'No,' Neeli said with a deep sigh.

'Let me die, Mother! He liked me very much. Listening to that song, about that woman's suffering, I feel consoled.'

Hesitantly, Neeli began to sing, to fulfill the last wish of a dying soul. But now the song lacked compassion; it carried no emotion. The sweet song that told of a fallen woman and was originally sung with a fair degree of artistic empathy by a poet who wandered around moonlit fields like an apparition – never before was it rendered so lifeless! There was no poetry in it, no emotion! And Neeli frequently missed certain lines as well.

Yet the fire that the song kindled in Chiruta's heart was a solace to her. She identified herself with the experiences of that poor sinful woman.

Neeli stopped singing and asked her, 'Who is it, then?'

'The white man.'

No one spoke for a long time. Even Neeli didn't try to console her in her mortal pain. No one agonized over her condition. And Chiruta didn't want it either.

She kept cursing and swearing.

'Chiruta, please stop it!' Ittiathi pleaded with her, deeply pained. And she said, with all the courage and clarity that she could muster, 'It's not you, man!'

Ittiathi was stunned. He felt as if a ball of fire had landed in his heart.

The hut shook.

Chiruta delivered herself of a baby.

'With me around,' Oroatha bragged, 'it never goes wrong.'

Neeli didn't even steal a glance at the baby. Ittiathi heard the baby's first cry, and he was dazed. He rose to his feet, moved over to the isolation hut and peeped in.

An unusually large baby. Brown hair. Light eyes. Fair complexion.

Ittiathi was stunned again. 'Chiruta!' He could hardly venture anything else.

'Yes?'

'What's this, dear?'

'Go away! This is not yours!'

Without a word Ittiathi slunk back to his hut and sat huddled on the veranda, watching the rolling waves on the vast expanse of water spreading far and wide.

The baby moved no more. It died.

'Ammachi!'

Neeli looked at her. Chiruta began to weep.

'I want to die!'

At the end of a severe bout of shivering, she died.

Translated by
Sudeepta

The Story of Kalyani

The very first building in Alappuzha belongs to Mutalali, the employer. It is almost a palace and he lives there. All the palatial buildings in the heart of the city belong to him. The chief market place and several shops are also his. All the feasts and parties that the city-dwellers remember were all hosted by him.

Mutalali has lands and shops in different parts of the city. Several orphanages and charitable institutions survive on his kindliness. At the temples in Ochira and Vaikkom he feeds the poor every month. Though his lands are many he does not get such a high income from them. His gains are not much from the landed property, but the charitable one does not seem to take it seriously. The people who live on his lands derive a fairly good income.

That is Rajayoga, the state of kingliness. He is almost perfect – except for that slight blemish. But can one call it a blemish? It is only a weakness. And the poor ones derive only benefit from this weakness. After all, great people must have a weakness or two!

Kalyani has come to Alappuzha with several intentions. She wants to stay somewhere on Mutalali's lands and get a job for her brother. It is the caretaker of Mutalali's landed property at Mavelikkara who has advised her to go to Alappuzha. He has even sent with her a letter to Pappu Pillai, Mutalali's caretaker here, recommending that she be given a place to stay somewhere in Mutalali's lands.

Kalyani has an old mother, a twelve-year old brother and a son who is one year old. She cannot get a convenient dwelling place in Mutalali's lands. Hence the small family settles down in another rented place in Alappuzha.

Her brother gets a job in some company or other in Alappuzha for five rupees a month. They get on well. If one asks how, it is not easy to reply. Such families are there in plenty in the city. A young woman would be the most important person in that family. She would be fairly good-looking, though her face might lack lustre. She would always be well dressed. The first impression she would give would be that of a well-to-do middle-class lady. She would be very talkative and would have several friends – even intimate friends. She would like all sorts of people. Nobody would say 'No' to her if she approaches them for help. Whatever she sets out to do, she sees to it that it is done.

In such families there may be an old mother or a boy. The lady of the house is their guardian. She gets angry with them and scolds them. They try to be very solicitous about her. If she has a child she will tell everybody that its father is either dead or divorced. Nobody would know the details.

If she goes to some place to get some things done, nobody would talk about her after she leaves. For, all that can be said about her has already been said; none has anything new to add. Sometimes someone may pass a comment such as: she looks tired nowadays.

Kalyani knows all the employees of Mutalali – knows them very well too. Through them she knows everything about Mutalali. She can even name the sweetmeat that he likes most. In her five years' stay in the city she has developed a new hobby: that is, to collect all the details about Mutalali's personal life. She can listen to stories about him for long hours and yet not be tired.

But Kalyani never has an eyeful of Mutalali. She has seen him go by in his car like a flash of lightning, that is all. Though it is five years since she came to Alappuzha, she has not realized all her dreams. She has not lived in Mutalali's lands. Everyday she talks to Pappu Pillai about it, but nothing has materialized so far.

Kalyani knows the advantages of living on a piece of land owned by Mutalali. Annakkutti and Meenakshi are her friends. They live one mile apart from each other, yet Meenakshi and Annakkutti hate each other. Both of them have told Kalyani the reason for their hatred. If Annakkutti wears a new jacket, Meenakshi becomes jealous. If Meenakshi puts on a new shawl, Annnakkuti will not sleep that night. Annakkutti, Meenakshi and so many others like them, enjoy several such privileges by staying in Mutalali's lands.

Mutalali has even gifted properties to some of them. If only she could meet Mutalali and manage to secure a place for herself too: Only Pappu Pillai can help her, but he doesn't oblige her at all!

She has come to the city seeking ways of bettering her life. Her anxiety keeps increasing as time goes by. How much longer must she wait? A hair on her head has turned grey. Today she is very confident about her abilities, but one year from today will she be so much sought after? All the dreams with which she set out from Mavelikkara are yet to be realized.

On a late, late night Kalyani and Pappu Pillai sit in her house, talking. Pappu Pillai is telling her the practical difficulties one by one.

Kalyani says: 'It can be done if you set your mind to it.'

Pappu Pillai shakes his head. He tells her that he is afraid the Mutalali might not like her at all. When he has beautiful young ladies, why should he like Kalyani?

Kalyani asks him: 'Do you think I'm worse than Annakkutti?'

'Don't ask me all that. It's very late. May I go?'

He gets up to leave and Kalyani follows him to the yard. She has decided to get it done at any cost. She too can do with ten cents of land. They continue their talk in the front yard. Kalyani cannot understand the argument that Mutalali might not like her. But she understands what is in Pappu Pillai's mind; she has seen so many people. She asks him: 'Chetta, tell me frankly what the obstacle is. You must tell me if it is not possible at all. You feel that Mutalali may not like me. But you haven't even tried it.'

Pappu Pillai responds: 'I haven't said it would not be possible at all. But... but... what can I do if you don't understand?'

'Tell me what it is.'

Pappu Pillai is silent for a while before he speaks: 'Alright, I shall tell you frankly. Why should I hide it? Now, why are you planning all this? So that you will ultimately gain something. Who knows, you may end up as my boss.'

'So?'

'You have to invest money to make money.'

Kalyani is relieved. Only now has she understood what is in Pappu Pillai's mind. Had she known it six years before, she could have fulfilled all her desires by now. She asks: 'How much do you demand, Chetta?'

'Since it's you, only ten rupees will do. After all, we have loved each other for six years, no?'

Kalyani goes inside and brings the money. Pappu Pillai accepts the ten rupees and tells her: 'I must tell you something more. You must hand over to me one-fourth of whatever Mutalali gives.'

Kalyani concedes, after thinking a bit.

Kalyani has her bath early. She ties her hair in a fashionable style and adorns it with flowers. She makes a dot mark on her forehead with saffron, chews betel leaves and rinses her mouth. When she looks at her well-dressed figure in the mirror, she is filled with pride.

She tells her mother that she will be late, for she is going for a movie. Her son cries out that he too wants to go with her but she drives him away. Kalyani goes out to the road after seeing a good omen.

A sweet fragrance wafts from her body as she sails by. Many people ask her: 'Hai, Mavelikkara, where are you going?'

'To see a movie.'

She has adorned herself for a special purpose that evening – to realize the ambition behind her coming to Alappuzha. No one understands it.

Pappu Pillai is there near the cinema. They talk for a while. Then Kalyani buys a ticket for the bench and enters.

Kalyani's mind shivers on seeing Annakkutti there. Meeting her rival at the most inconvenient spot!

As usual, Annakkutti starts talking about Meenakshi. Kalyani starts hating Annakkutti.

The movie begins. Though Annakkutti stops talking, Kalyani cannot concentrate on the movie. She is thinking of the auspicious time ahead. Suppose Mutalali does not like her! She closes her eyes and prays to the goddess of Chettikulangara. If only she succeeds…! If she succeeds she will take her revenge on Pappu Pillai and drive him out of Alappuzha.

It is hot inside the cinema and she starts sweating. What a nuisance! Suppose the sweat stinks! Will she be able to wash her body before seeing Mutalali? Then she must change her dress too! As she sits worrying thus, she sees Pappu Pillai in between the dark curtains and goes out. Annakkutti grasps the situation and she too comes out.

She sees Kalyani and Pappu Pillai entering the car parked under a tree on the road south to the park.

~

The car stops in front of Kalyani's house after midnight. Kalyani and Pappu Pillai get down from it. Pappu Pillai hands her a five-rupee note. Kalyani takes it but stands stunned. Pappu Pillai asks: 'What's the matter?'

'What is this, Chetta?'

'That's all there is.'

Kalyani grits her teeth and suppresses her anger. Pappu Pillai does not see it in the darkness. All the promises made by Mutalali, blind with emotion, resound in her ears. What clownish acts he had been up to! Had knelt at her feet! Asked her to kill him! And then five rupees! Mutalali may not even know about it. This traitor is tricking both of them. Her mind prepares another plan. She needn't quarrel with this demon; but he must be driven out of Alappuzha.

She goes to her house and the car speeds by.

Days pass. Women who dwell on Mutalalai's lands come to know of a new rival. Everyday Kalyani expects the arrival of Pappu Pillai but he is not to be seen. One day she sees him near Mutalali's shop.

'What's this, Chetta, I haven't seen you for so long!'

'I couldn't come. So busy, you know. There's no time for anything.'

She calls him to a corner where they can be alone and asks him: 'Mutalali asked me to come the next day too. Why didn't you come to take me?'

'O, Mutalali didn't like you.'

Kalyani is shocked. The promises Mutalali made stuck out their tongues at her. Mutalali had told her that he had never experienced such pleasure; that Annakkutti and Meenakshi were old prunes! Kalyani decides that this traitor is lying. He wants more money to be the go-between! She suppresses her anger and asks: 'If so, why did he ask me to come again the next day?' Pappu Pillai cannot help laughing.

'My dear Kalyani, did you believe those words? Was he conscious then? He may say so many things at such times… to put other people in difficulty.'

That was true. Mutalali was quite drunk. What should she believe? Kalyani says again: 'No, Chetta, that won't do. That day I was a bit bewildered. Give me one more opportunity.'

'Let me see. Maybe, the day after tomorrow. Tomorrow I shall come to your house.'

Translated by
B. Chandrika

From Karachi…

Two street urchins came out of the backyard of the hotel and walked on, arm in arm along the road. They were seen there everyday at that time. One was a Muslim, the other, a Hindu. Both were always seen together, inseparable companions. And they slept together – beneath the lamp post at a crossroads, nestling against each other.

A forlorn street urchin got another beggar boy as his companion near the garbage bin behind the hotel. He helped him drive away the dog about to leap into the garbage bin. The leftovers in the bin were more than enough for the two. Thus they became friends. One got a piece of bone, and the other a piece of potato. They pooled them as common property and shared it equally between them. One got a little rice and the other a little curry. And when they put them together, they both had a sumptuous feast! That they had to continue the fight with their common enemy became their joint responsibility, which held them together. It was as if one dog had brought two others on the scene.

And thus they lived on. They had something to eat, and they had sound sleep. What else did they need?

One had the other to depend on, and the latter, the former. An inseparable relationship. For a man, whether he be a beggar or a murderer, there must be someone as his bosom companion.

One day the Hindu urchin was asked by his Muslim companion: 'Who named you Krishnakumar?'

Admitting his ignorance, Krishnakumar asked in return, 'Well, who named you Abdullah?'

Abdullah too was at a complete loss.

And that made them laugh for a long time.

Krishnakumar asked how these names came to be used. Abdullah did not know. Is a child born with a name? Abdullah answered in the negative. But Abdullah had another question: how did they come to the earth? Born to whom? Evidently, born to two women. And after the delivery, what did the women do? Thus their enquiry went on. Abdullah would end the enquiry saying: 'Perhaps those women are dead. Even if they are somewhere here, we may not recognise them.'

Krishnakumar disagreed: 'If they are still alive we should track them down, and ask them why they gave birth to us.'

Thus continued their search for information.

Public meetings and processions were then taking place all over the country. Streets were patrolled by policemen armed with lathis and guns. And they opened fire wherever meetings were held. No one was allowed in the streets after eight in the night. Even so, the two street urchins slept beneath the lamp post.

The beggar boys also somehow knew that all the meetings and processions were to drive the white men out of India.

As Krishnakumar woke up one day, he did not find Abdullah near him. He shouted his name, and waited for him. No, he was not there. The time when the meals were served in the hotel was fast approaching. Where was Abdullah?

Before he ate his share he set aside for Abdullah a portion of what he could collect from the garbage bin. When would he return? Nobody knew. If he came long after the meal-time...?

On that day, Krishnakumar had to fight three dogs single-handedly. As they saw he was alone, they growled and barked at him. And once they almost managed to wrest from him the portion of leftovers he had put aside for Abdullah. Thank God, only a piece of bone had been lost to the dogs.

A little later Abdullah came running. He had a lot of things to tell his friend. He was quite impatient to unburden himself. With anger and joy, Krishnakumar asked him where he had been. Abdullah did not seem to be in a mood to answer the question. And he blurted out, quite excitedly.

'You have seen the mansion at the junction... the mudalali (rich man) there also bears my name, Abdullah!...'

Krishnakumar drove away the flies from the crumbs he had kept for Abdullah. He has been trying to keep the flies away for a long time now. But Abdullah did not seem to notice his friend's gesture.

Krishnakumar asked: 'Have you had any food?'

'I am hungry...'

He began to eat the leftovers. Very excited, he continued:

'I heard mudalali's speech. We, the Muslims, are going to get a nation of our own. Pakistan Zindabad.'

Abdullah was beside himself with happiness. There was a meeting, a big procession. And he took part in both. Seeing Abdullah's excitement, Krishnakumar felt rather sad. Abdullah had gone leaving him alone; he had involved himself in many things; he may have eaten elsewhere. True, his love for Krishnakumar had been on the decline. He seemed to have forgotten Krishnakumar. And Krishnakumar questioned him, rather searchingly.

Abdullah explained everything with excitement. He did not seem to think that he had done anything wrong. When they were asleep on the railway platform the other day, a few people came in procession to receive some important leader who was to arrive by the night train. The processionists garlanded the leader, and there was much excitement. Abdullah tried his best to wake up Krishnakumar, but he could not as the latter was sound asleep. Abdullah followed the procession.

Krishnakumar asked: 'Did you get any food?'

'Rice. A big feast. Also sakkath (alms)...'

Krishnakumar was downcast.

'That's bad. You could have taken me also.'

'No, it was only for us, the Muslims.'

Tears welled up in Krishnakumar's eyes. He had only one relative in the world: Abdullah. And Abdullah had gone to the feast all alone. And what is more, he had not brought him even a gingelly cake!

'I have kept this for you. I know your love for me. However, eat this...'

Abdullah regretted his lapse: he should have brought Krishnakumar something.

He said: 'Next time I'll bring you half of what I get ...'

Krishnakumar butted in: 'That means you'll again go alone, without me!'

Now and then Abdullah disappeared, and returned after two or three days.

A sense of loneliness slowly overcame Krishnakumar. He thought that Abdullah would one day disappear for ever. And he had to fight the dogs all alone; had to sleep alone. And there would be nobody to speak to, to lean against. He waited for Abdullah's return whenever the latter left. And Abdullah did not appear to be much worried about being away from his one-time close friend.

During that period Abdullah got a good dhoti. Once or twice, he had money too. Half the dhoti was readily given to Krishnakumar. And he did not spend the entire money on his own. Abdullah now had to tell his friend something new about which Krishnakumar refused to comment. Abdullah was always waxing eloquent about Abdullah mudalali, and the kingdom (nation) that was to be carved out for the Muslims. There, in that nation of Muslims, there would not be any starvation, or any beggars. It would be the kingdom of Allah. Sometimes, Abdullah fell into a pensive mood. And then Krishnakumar felt that Abdullah was distancing himself. He felt alienated. True, Abdullah had something else as well to think about; he had known Abdullah mudalali...

With tearful eyes Krishnakumar nestled against the garbage bin. He too has something to think about – his solitude. He felt rather nervous being with Abdullah as in the past.

One day a proud Abdullah declared that he had seen the interior of Abdullah mudalali's mansion. He began to expand upon his visit with a sense of pride. Angry and sad, Krishnakumar retorted: 'I too have seen the interior of the mansion of the zamindar, my namesake.'

Abdullah disputed: 'Oh, that's nothing when compared with this mansion.'

'Who told you? It's better, bigger...'

Abdullah was getting more and more obstinate. And Krishnakumar was not prepared to yield.

Abdullah retorted: 'Your zamindar is a kafer.'

'And your mudalali is an untouchable.'

With uncontrollable anger Abdullah stood up and shouted: 'Pakistan Zindabad.'

Krishnakumar thumbed his nose at him, and Abdullah tried to beat Krishnakumar. And then they were engaged in fisticuffs...

~

16 June 1947. The die was cast on the future of India. Pakistan was to be born on 15 August 1947. Abdullah conveyed the special news to Krishnakumar: 'I am going to Karachi.'

Krishnakumar was taken aback. 'Why are you going?'

'That's our nation, our kingdom.'

'Then, whose is this nation?'

'This is yours.'

Krishnakumar kept mum. He had no one. No one to remember him. His food he would continue to find in the garbage bin behind the hotel. He could sleep on the footpath. But ... but... the but that speaks volumes for the noble human sentiments... I will not speak to any one, I will seek the bone pieces in the garbage bin, Krishnakumar thought.

Abdullah was still eloquent about Karachi.

With tearful eyes Krishnakumar asked: 'Abdullah, shall I come with you?'

'No, no. Muslims alone are allowed there.'

'Then, who do I have?'

Krishnakumar burst into tears. And that cry went straight to Abdullah's heart. It was his own friend, one who always waited for him. True, when I leave he will have no companion. Abdullah too was sad.

He gently caressed Krishnakumar, and said: 'Should we always be like this, street urchins… ?'

'I shall return from Karachi a rich man. The money I make is not mine alone. You'll also have a share in it. Don't cry, my friend…'

Abdullah wiped Krishnakumar's tears.

The dawn of August. The beggar boy somehow managed to collect a Turkish cap, a shirt and pyjamas. In his new attire, Abdullah seemed to Krishnakumar a very important person. He was no longer his one-time companion near the hotel garbage bin.

Abdullah looked at Krishnakumar, from the train that moved out of the station, bound for Pakistan. The train disappeared from Krishnakumar's view…

Krishnakumar was at his wits' end. He felt miserably lonely. A sense of fear gripped him as he realized that there would be no one for him to turn to…

15 August as well as the Punjab massacre was over. Krishnakumar was compelled to think that it was good that Abdullah had left for Karachi. Otherwise, he might also have been butchered in the massacre.

A street urchin in torn pyjamas and rags could be seen walking away from the hotel garbage bin in a town in East Punjab.

He still slept on the footpath. He never uttered a word to anyone as if he had no tongue. One thing he did without fail: whenever the train from Karachi reached the station, he was on the platform.

This waiting continued for years. Everyday the beggar boy waited for the train from Karachi. Though the business in the hotel had declined, and the garbage bin had turned rusty, he still fed himself from it.

And one day when he reached the rear side of the hotel, he saw someone with a swollen body lying near the garbage bin. It was Abdullah. He was too weak to get up.

Krishnakumar sat near him, placed his head on his lap, caressed and kissed his friend, and burst into tears.

Abdullah had come in search of his only friend to die in his lap. And the hotel garbage bin was perhaps the most appropriate place for him to die in, in his friend's arms.

Translated by
G.N. Panikkar

Death of Gandhiji

Our village was wiped off the face of the earth. Who died, who survived, what happened to whom – I do not know. Somehow I escaped. And there was no one else on that road. Perhaps I am the sole survivor – spared to tell the story of that ruined village.

I walked on, without food, without seeing the face of a single human being. There was the debris of arson and murder on the road, of which, what left the deepest impression on my mind was an amputated hand. I think it was a young woman's hand.

By the evening of the fifth day, I was totally exhausted. Yet I walked on. Not that there was any strength left in my legs; I just kept walking, that's all. I didn't feel as though I had escaped; nor did I feel the possibility of escape. I just went on like a machine; no intelligence, no reason, no consciousness.

'Son!'

A voice pierced my ears like a whistle. I was dazed. Then I regained consciousness. I am a human being. Born in a village in West Bengal. I had a house there. And a mother who called me 'Son'. I recollected that much in a trice. The next moment I saw a sword shining above the lowered head of an old woman.

Again the cry: 'My son!' And I responded: 'Yes?' Perhaps my mother was not dead!

My heart began to beat faster. Perhaps my younger brother and sister were there with her. Where was she calling from?

'Mother!'

'Son!'

Then I felt that I should not call out aloud. I had still not crossed the danger zone.

An old woman's hands – reduced to mere bones – embraced me. She placed her hands on my shoulder and cried, sobbing: 'Son! O my son!' and I could just mutter: 'Mother!'

My mother could not have escaped in the half-moment that it took the shining sword to come down… And I felt greatly relieved!

Thus I got a mother, and the old woman a son. She had seen her son being torn to pieces; yet she too, like me, felt relieved.

We walked on. She asked me where we were going. She wanted to go to the place where Bapuji lived. She would have nothing to fear there!

Next day, in the evening, a young woman joined us as my sister and the old woman's daughter. In the same way as I had found my mother and she, her son. And the next day we got a four-year-old brother from a village that had been razed to the ground. I don't know how he had escaped. He was perhaps just a blot that escaped those bloody sinners' eyes.

On the seventh day an elder brother joined us. 'Joined' would not be the right word. We just came across this tall, fat man. A Hindu, he had a long sword in his hands. Thinking he was a refugee like the rest of us, Mother named him as her eldest son and our brother.

On the ninth morning we reached a place where our brother suddenly stopped. Then a great roaring cry that seemed to rise from the bottom of the earth: 'Harsanker Mahadev!'

We were astounded. I looked at the tall man, and then I realized who, or what he was. A gentle smile lit up Mother's toothless mouth. Our sister gave a deep sigh. At a distance we saw a flag fluttering in the sky. It was the Union flag.

We were in India. The land of Bapuji, I said to my mother. Our brother gave me a look, and his eyes rolled meaningfully. As if to protest what I had said, he roared: 'Harsanker Mahadev!'

We had heard a similar roar in Pakistan: 'Allah-O Akbar!' The terror and intensity of that cry was similar to that of our brother. This too would terrify the people.

~

We shouldn't have headed for the refugee camp. We should have just walked on, mortally afraid, till the end of our lives. Then we could have escaped the heart-rending memories of the past. As the need for security dawned on me, memories of the past became clearer. Where was my mother? Where was my little brother? My younger sister? Sister, who had lost everything, began to weep. The brother cried and wanted to know where he could find his mother. And Mother would at times say that none of their folks were dead, that they would meet them soon and go back home with them. Bapuji was still alive, wasn't he? So everyone could go back home one day. But at other times, she would start weeping.

Was it possible to wipe off our past lives just like that? I had lived for twenty-eight years, and I was not to see again a single face that I had been familiar with. And the old woman had to begin a new life at the age of eighty-two.

Thus we had to begin a new life in a new world all over again. Mother embraced the three of us in the folds of her emaciated arms and said, her eyes brimming with tears: 'We are a family, my children.'

Yes, we felt it. We were a family.

Our little brother jumped into Mother's lap.

~

At the refugee camp I asked Mother how on that fateful night, she had made bold to call out aloud to me. What if I had been a Muslim?

Mother replied: 'Individually, no one hates anyone. Even if you were a Muslim, you wouldn't have harmed me.'

She had seen me on the tenth day after she had left her village. Meanwhile a Muslim family had given her shelter for a couple of days. But that family itself was under a threat precisely for that reason. So she had left them.

Mother concluded our conversation thus: 'I wonder how all these things have come about. People who have been living together for generations are now cutting one another's throats. How did this misfortune come about?'

She told me a few heart-warming stories of Hindu-Muslim friendship. Stories that speak of a unity that could harvest gold from the fields of West Punjab, stories that go on and on through generations!

The man whom Mother had brought into our family as our elder brother (Gowrisanker was his name) had not been seen for five or six days. She began to get worried.

I could guess where he might be. He might have gone to massacre the innocent Muslims in Eastern Punjab. His sword must have drunk the blood of innumerable innocents. But I did not say anything about it to Mother.

She began to cry the next day. She wanted me to tell her why her son hadn't come back. What doubts she had! She wanted to die after entrusting me to a strong brother.

He came back the next day. There were signs of his having carried out a massive destruction. A cruel smile of satisfaction played on his face. The satisfaction of having avenged the wrong done to us.

He told me he had finished off fifty 'low-borns'! I was stunned. What a cruel beast he was! Then I wanted to know more about him.

He belonged to an organization which worked toward saving the Hindu religion. I was dumbfounded when I heard the names of the leaders and patrons of the organization. People whom we revered! Great leaders whom we expected would bring peace and prosperity to the country! Inmates at Gandhiji's ashram and those who followed his footsteps!

'So this is being done with Gandhiji's knowledge?' I asked.

'Is Gandhiji an obstacle?'

I couldn't ask him anything more. How could I believe what he said? A disciple who used to get worried over Gandhiji's health whenever he went on a fast to uphold communal amity – was it possible to believe that this disciple of Gandhiji would hand over to Gowrisanker a sword with which to slay the Muslims? Perhaps it was true! After all, he was a wealthy man; and he would perhaps indulge in such double-dealing!

'Maybe you don't like these things, eh?' Gowrisanker asked me.

I gave him a hollow smile, and said: 'Isn't this a betrayal of that holy soul?'

I looked into his face intently. Suddenly there was a change of expression there. Not hate, not enmity, not even annoyance or frustration over Gandhiji's grief; it was the expression of one who was beset by a thousand grave secrets that he carried within himself. He knew a lot about the existing system and what was going on behind the scenes. And he had a lot to say in reply to my question concerning Gandhiji.

'To put it briefly, brother,' he said. 'Gandhiji is a saint, a yogi. But he has betrayed the Hindu religion.'

Then he began his narration with Naukhali. He severely condemned Gandhiji's hunger campaigns, saying they succeeded only in turning the Hindus into a pack of sheep while the Muslims remained unchanged!

Gowrisanker sincerely believed in what he said. Undoubtedly, it was his firm conviction that the Muslims did not deserve to live. I wondered if he would ultimately say that Gandhiji himself was a Muslim!

'In that case why should we blame the Muslims of Pakistan? Where does the reason for it all lie?'

After listening to him, I said: 'I have come here not because I think this is a Hindu nation. Not because I think this is paradise or that life will be peaceful and secure here. Not even because it was possible to call this the country of my origin. I am here only because Bapuji lives here.'

Gowrisanker just gave a meaningful 'hm'.

Mother was in a hurry to see Bapuji. And sister too. How many stories about Gandhiji were doing the rounds among the refugees! It was said that he could, with his divine eye, locate stolen daughters and absconding relatives! He was also said to be in communion with the dead! Narrating these stories, Mother said: 'In Delhi there is a bungalow owned by a millionaire. Gandhiji is now put up there. People say that during his next fasting ritual he will die a yogic death and attain salvation. He will not remain on earth for long. So we should go and see him as fast as we can.

Here, too, Gowrisanker's hand could be seen.

We obtained permission to go to Delhi. We set out on the journey by a train that was heavily guarded.

We were moving away from the land of our birth. I looked at the vast expanses of the land that was going to be our country. This too had been our motherland. One fine morning there had come a judgement which said 'No.' And we were refugees in our own country.

The size of my stomach, my craze for fashionable clothing, my stubbornness – all that was now to be suffered by the thirty crore people of this country. Yes, I had to be fed, clothed, and finally given six feet of earth.

The train left the industrial zone and sped along the plains. Our sister's words brought me back from my thoughts.

'See, brother, how abundantly wheat and paddy grow here!' she said. 'We won't have to starve!'

And Mother asked, looking at the smoke-pipes rising to the sky at a distance: 'That's where they weave clothes?'

'Yes,' said our sister.

I started thinking: Aren't there people who starve here? The country we have left behind also had fertile fields. But it was a land of utter poverty.

'The wheat that grows in these fields is not for us to eat,' I said. 'The clothes that are woven in those mills are not for us to wear.'

'Then, aren't these meant for the people?'

'No, Mother! Those millionaires who have put up Bapuji in their bungalows – they're the ones who decide.'

'So, my son, is this place too like our country? Is it being ruled by merciless zamindars and other masters?'

'Yes.'

'But there's Bapuji here.'

'Mother,' I said. 'They tried putting up Bapuji in their bungalows, giving him money. But it was of no use. Bapuji continues to think of the poor. So now they have made him a kind of prisoner.'

Suddenly I felt that I shouldn't have said it. Our life depended on India's generosity. And I was speaking against the lord of the land. Did anyone hear me…?

~

The city where Bapuji lived! Everyone on the train was overjoyed. Now we were safe. But even in that city how many people would be there who were afraid for their lives? Gowrisanker had arrived there with his long sword.

I went round the city of Delhi and saw its varied sights. A city of diverse experiences! A city ruled by innumerable emperors over the ages! A city that saw the fall of many thrones and dynasties! From the author or Bhagavad Gita down to Bapuji – all had blessed the city with their presence.

I felt that the city was submerged in a shadow of gloom. I could sense the deep sigh of olden days. Yes, what the city had to tell were stories of destruction. And you could feel your enthusiasm being drained. The city was in fear of the future. Its memory was fresh with tales from its prehistoric days. Lion-hearted emperors had turned to dust on its soil. Innumerable crowns and sceptres that had been praised and treasured were flying about the city's sky as mere dust. The city was haunted by the spectres of the past.

A few long streets in Delhi would remind you of the time of the Mughal emperors who had brought glory to India. And as I walked along those streets I felt as if I were behind time by about two centuries.

I was soon overpowered by another thought. Any Muslim walking that street would feel that he was the lord of this country. When it was necessary to fight a foreign power, a Muslim leader pointed out to the Muslim youth those streets, as well as the Qutab Minar and the Taj Mahal, and said: 'Your ancestors ruled here.' And the Hindu leader, who stood shoulder to shoulder with him exhorted the Hindu youth to remember the great Hindu emperors and Hindu culture and civilization and said, 'This country is yours.' Soon the foreign power left. The Muslim youth and the Hindu youth drew inspiration from the lessons they had learned from their leaders; they argued with each other saying, 'This is mine, this is mine', and finally they drew their daggers. What else could cause the sheer intensity of the Pakistani Muslim's belief that the Hindu had no right to live as well as of the Hindu Indian's belief that the Muslim had no right to live? Could those leaders be held responsible for this? Who knows... ? Let history pass the judgement.

~

Birla Mandir! Taller than the neighbouring buildings, it stood with its head held high in the sky. It had a certain dignity, a high-born élan, and it was far more important than the residence of the Viceroy. Yet... yet, somehow, to me it seemed to be a prison.

Soon I was led into Gandhiji's presence, and I paid my loving tribute to him. I felt a lightness of being which was unprecedented.

What I saw was completely different from what I had expected! The image of Gandhiji in my mind had a halo around him; he had eyes that shone with a divine power and authority. I had seen him in the guise of Vishnu riding the eagle, and I had seen him with a third eye on his brow.

But it was a human being who stood before me now. A man who opened his mouth and laughed innocently whenever I was in tears! I could talk about my needs; I could confess my sinful deeds. For Bapuji was someone who loved me.

May the thunderbolt fall upon the heads of those terrible sinners who had made a god out of my Bapuji! What tricks and tactics they had employed for the purpose! They had got poets to sing in praise of him. They had painters to draw pictures of him. They even had a few dry and hollow men construct obscure interpretations of whatever Bapuji told us, sharing in our mirth and joy, correcting us with grief whenever we went astray, and advising us on the little problems of our everyday life. And they called it 'Gandhian Philosophy!' Whatever Gandhiji said could be understood by the forty-crore Indians. For it was all about things that mattered to them. There was no need for an interpretation. But the 'Masters' of those interpreters did not want the poor to understand what Gandhiji was saying.

No, it was nothing new. The world had seen the same thing happen before. The mendicant of love who was crucified at Calvary 2000 years ago was turned into the Son of God. What he said too was given a series of interpretations. He was portrayed as a very handsome young man in the pictures they drew of him. And many a false poem was written about him. And the result? Today that man was beyond the grasp of human beings.

Why take such pains to make a god out of my Bapuji? Why couldn't he be treated as a human being? There was something there; there indeed was a need, a reason.

There was something that spread the light of vitality and love of life in the hearts of the beggar and the downtrodden in every nook and corner of India. Love for Bapuji! That love aroused their sense of freedom. And there were some people who were terrified. If that love was not transformed – their interests were at stake. When Gandhiji was turned into the eagle-borne Vishnu, when his sayings were turned into divine utterances, the god of freedom was transformed into the god who had already become an instrument in the hands of the master and the zamindar. And the sense of freedom that had been aroused in millions of people was thus frozen.

I saw the working of a great machine. In the working of that great machine India was torn into two in a moment. But some of the vital nerves were yet to break. They were stretched taut, causing an intense pain. In the working of the same machine the Mahatma became a prisoner. The long sword carried by Gowrisanker was part of that machine. And the superstitious beliefs that arose among the refugees were also the result of the working of that machine.

~

I took a walk around the sprawling complex; the building was quite an eyeful. Those smart guys had not built a prison-house for Gandhiji; they had, instead, made a prisoner of him where he stayed. The power and influence of the owner of various mills and extensive fields was at work everywhere. The poor man had gone as far as 'Bhangikkalini'. But there too he had been a prisoner. You know why his disciples made a god out of Gandhiji? To gag the millions of poor Indians. Could one possibly go against a disciple of Gandhiji? And to imagine the publicity worth thousands of pounds that the Birla Mandir received because Gandhiji was staying there!

Back at the refugee camp Mother asked me anxiously: 'You saw Bapuji?'

'Yes.'

There was something peculiar about her anxiety.

'I want to see him immediately.'

'Mother, you look worried.'

'Yes. Bapuji has completed the mission of his life. Now he can die at will.'

'Completed the mission! Bapuji will live till a 120.'

'No. Every incarnation, once the life-mission is over, will merge with the Cause.'

What could I tell the old woman!

~

30 January. The accursed, fateful day! Bapuji couldn't be seen any more!

Mother couldn't see him. At the refugee camp fear and helplessness were writ large on every face. Their guardian angel was gone.

I went into our tent and found Mother listening intently to Gowrisanker.

'And how about Bhagvan Parthasarathy? The huntsman's arrow became a cause, that's all. A cause only for the people of the world to talk about!'

Mother was convinced. Yet she couldn't bear it. And Gowrisanker came up with another interpretation. He recited the verse from the Bhagvad Gita beginning 'Sambhavami Yuge Yuge' – what will happen, will happen. The interpretation centred on 'happening'. 'Not to be' was also a happening. So Gandhiji was said to have made 'not to be' happen to him so that dharma was established!

I couldn't take it any longer. Gowrisanker saw me. He couldn't look me in the eye. Apparently afraid that I would do something, he kept his eye on me and rose to his feet. And then he ran like a dog.

The hefty fellow was a real coward though he had the sword with him. I didn't understand the meaning of that cowardice.

~

At the Raj Ghat, today, people pay their homage, pray and offer floral tributes; they walk round the mausoleum chanting mantras. And there is a priest too.

Those wealthy masters and zamindars often visit the refugee camp. The shadow of a fear is reflected in their eyes. Not the fear of guilt, though. They are, in fact, hatching a few schemes in their own devious ways.

The sense of freedom aroused by Bapuji in the forty crore Indians is still raging. The wealthy masters know; they understand. Having imprisoned Bapuji, they have so far been hiding behind his shadow. Now, who is there to control the forty crore's desire for freedom that can turn into a revolution? In there any way the floodgates could be shut tight? This is what they fear every moment.

Perhaps it's true. Perhaps Bapuji's death was for the good of the forty crores. He had loved us. Our sufferings had set his heart on fire. But the prisoner who had yearned to convert the wealthy master had, in fact, been dampening the natural rebelliousness of the poor. Will the master have a change of heart? Even if it's possible, will the whole system change? Gandhiji was an obstacle on the path to such a transformation.

Yet, what disappeared from our view was a figure all of us loved.

Translated by
V.C. Harris

The Boundary Dispute

The land lying waste in between the two plots on the east and the west must be about four cents. In the first year it was only a grassland; in the second year it turned into a shrub-ground. Today, two or three trees including a banyan and a jack, flourish there. People who are familiar with the history of the place find the trees to be growing with a wild strength and determination. When its history began, there was not even a single blade of grass.

Now it has become a small forest with grass, shrubs and intertwining vines. Even venomous snakes are found inside the thick growth. They hatch eggs and breed more snakes. People say that this four cents of land may create history again. It definitely has a supernatural aura about it.

On the south and the north of this land there are two other pieces of land. Without proper maintenance and clearing, the grass from the land lying waste has encroached into them too. A dilapidated house stands in each of these plots, small houses almost falling to pieces. The people who live in them also look drained of life and spirit.

These two pieces of land belonged to two hard-working farmers of healthy physique. They used to get from the land fruitful yields for their hard labour. Not even the space of a spade was left uncultivated. They had cultivated almost every crop – colocasia, yam, peas, potatoes, chilly. The huts that now bowed low with broken rafters stood erect then. The roofs, unthatched and leaking now, were then level and polished. The two houses enjoyed hard-earned prosperity.

Pappu Nair, the farmer who owned the house to the south, had a son, Raman. The true son of his father, Raman was fat, chubby and smart. Chacko, the farmer who owned the northern house, also had a son: Authakkutti, more or less like Raman in appearance. They were friends, studying in the same class.

One day they came home from school as usual, hand in hand and talking. They were puzzled to see the crowd that had gathered to the north of Pappu Nair's house, that is, to the south of Chacko's house. The boys ran to the spot together. They saw Chacko lying dead in a pool of blood, his head cut off at the neck. Pappu Nair, holding a blood-stained knife, stood there in a frenzy of anger, blood splashed all over his body. Authakkutti's mother, held by some people, was screaming loudly.

It was the dispute over the boundary of their plots of land that aggravated the quarrel that ended in Chacko's death. The quarrel was for just four cents of land! The people who gathered round were afraid to go near Pappu Nair.

Raman and Authakkutti stood near each other looking on. Had Authakkutti realized that his father was dead? And was Raman afraid to go near his father? Pappu Nair and Chacko had quarrelled with each other and one had killed the other – all for their children! But the children were standing together. Would they move away from each other once they learnt the truth?

The police came, made the inquest and arrested the murderer. Authakkutti did not go to school the next day, for he had to go to the church for his father's burial. Raman too did not go to school though he had nothing particular to do.

Authakkutti never spoke to Raman after that. Raman too did not speak to him. Both of them knew that Authakkutti had been made fatherless by Raman's father. Their ways parted, though not deliberately. Though they were kids their minds might have felt heavy. They were not old enough to hate each other. May be Authakkutti wanted to ask Raman, 'But Raman, how could your father kill my father? After all, how could he?'

The reason why Raman turned his head and walked off on seeing Authakkutti was that maybe he was unable to stand the unasked question.

When time passed and they grew up, wouldn't it be possible that Authakkutti may feel like avenging the death of his father?

Pappu Nair's wife had cried out wildly when the police arrested him and took him away. After that day, Raman never saw his father. Pappu Nair never came out of prison. He was sentenced to death by hanging.

Raman's mother was informed of the date of hanging. Raman also came to know of it. That night his mother sobbed aloud, beating her chest hysterically. The noise must have reached the neighbouring house too. Perhaps it was heard in the prison in Thiruvananthapuram which was so far away. Was Chacko's wife happy to hear the cries of Pappu Nair's wife?

But why should she be happy? Could Chacko come back to life if Pappu Nair was hanged? Could that gap ever be filled? How would she be consoled if Nani too were to be made a widow and Raman rendered fatherless? What was lost was lost for ever.

How can anyone know the workings of the human mind? On hearing of Pappu Nair's hanging, Chacko's wife must have experienced a coolness along with the pain of the reopened wound.

Anyway the chapter was closed thus. Both the families were orphaned. The two pieces of fertile land of good yield slowly turned grassy. Authakkutti and Raman were brought up by their mothers. Both the boys had enough cause to grieve, and perhaps some cause to complain to each other too.

That was how the four cents of land in between the two plots became a miniature forest. It was nobody's land. Even though his father's blood was split there, Authakkutti was afraid to claim it. Raman was equally fearful. Meanwhile the trees grew; would the expensive timber pave the way for the next quarrel?

Raman and Authakkutti passed their adolescence. Even then they did not speak to each other. Was it because they hated each other?

Perhaps yes; perhaps no! Maybe they could not speak to each other because of their memories of the past.

Slowly the two plots of land became green and fertile. The two youths could be seen tilling their lands, restoring to the earth her lost prosperity. Authakkutti repaired his house and soon Raman too did the maintenance work on his house.

Yet the four cents of waste land lay unclaimed. But now the shrubs were not allowed to extend beyond its boundary.

One night Raman was coming back home from the market. It was a narrow lane with high mud walls on both sides, not wide enough for two people to pass at the same time. Someone was coming from the other end of the lane towards Raman. It was Authakkutti!

Raman stopped abruptly, shocked to the marrow. Authakkutti also stopped. There was about twenty-five feet between them. Neither of them took a step forward. It was the first time they were meeting alone like this. What all must have passed through their minds as they stood in fear, confronting each other! Certainly the same memories… and the same pictures. Wouldn't they have thought of the same sight that greeted them when they returned hand in hand from school? The long, pathetic wails of Authakkutti's mother! As if in continuation, the cries of Raman's mother that echoed on a night – equally long and pathetic! All these thoughts must have crossed their minds. They saw the same images… the same facts… but saw them differently. One could blame the other; each could have his own arguments against the other too!

Authakkutti and Raman did not possess any weapons. But each of them thought that the other had some weapon. Each wished he had a weapon, not for attacking the other, but for self-defence. Both of them must have thought of pulling out a stone from the mud wall or even of walking forward bravely. But neither moved; they stood still, rooted to the spot.

Suddenly both of them turned round and started running away from each other – at the same time!

The mother asked the son who reached home running and panting: 'What happened Authakkutti, my son?'

Authakkutti was so upset that he could not even utter a word. The mother became frantic, beating her breasts, and asked, 'Tell me son, tell me what happened.'

The same scene was being enacted in the next house too!

After his sweat and panting subsided a little, Authakkutti told his mother what had happened. The mother's hair stood on end due to fear. The son of the devil who had severed the neck of an innocent human being! Had he lunged at Authakkutti and…! She couldn't even think of it.

She murmured: 'Had he come near you…'

Authakkutti told her, 'I was on my guard though I had no weapon.'

The mother heaved a sigh and said, 'Jesus has saved you, my son!'

The more she thought of it, the more fearful she became. She was afraid of the future. How could they get out of their house if this state of affairs continued? Would they be safe even if they stayed indoors? Helplessly the mother said, 'They were the ones who murdered a man in cold blood. What have we done to them? Yet they are against us.'

That was her viewpoint: it was Pappu Nair who caused them harm. She continued – 'Are we responsible for his death on the gallows?'

She could not understand why the ire had to be carried over to the next generation.

In the next house too the mother asked the son what had happened as he rushed in panting and sweating. The son described the fearful incident and she said helplessly, 'If his father had been murdered, the person who did it had ended in the gallows. Why are they still angry?'

The mother asked the son not to stir out of the house, for Authakkutti might be stalking him. 'You are saved now only by the grace of God.'

Raman told her: 'I was on my guard, though I had no weapon.'

In both the houses the people were thinking of ways of living without fear.

The news flashed across the village the next day. Some people said that Raman had tried to attack Authakkutti; some said it was the other way round.

The wrong committed by the previous generation was being carried over.

For self-defence, Raman and Authakkutti had knives made secretly. Their mothers did not know about it; they did not tell the mothers at all.

~

The banyan and the jacks became huge trees. Fruits started appearing on the jack trees. On one tree there were so many fruits that the tree appeared overwhelmed with the burden. Authakkutti and Raman used to count the fruits, each taking care that the other did not see him counting. From the look of the fruits, they seemed to belong to the varikka family – an extremely sweet variety.

Who would take those jackfruits? Several people in the village discussed the question. Whose head is destined to roll in blood again under the jack trees? Will the other person too end up in the gallows? That tree had sprung from the soil on which Chacko's blood lay in puddles. Hence, they said, the tree's plentiful fruition!

One day an enormous fruit fell from the tree, overripe. No one laid claim to it. The birds feasted on the fruit. Not a pip was taken by anybody.

Both the families thought of the waste.

Another jackfruit became overripe. Soon it too would fall down and be useless. Raman, who looked at the tree, exclaimed aloud: 'How sad that no man can enjoy these fruits!'

His own voice startled him. Had anybody overheard him? He regained his courage the next minute. Let anybody hear – even Authakkutti – for what he uttered was only the truth. The blessings of nature were being destroyed, untouched and unused.

The second fruit also fell off and became food for the birds. Honey-sweet fruit! But nobody took even the pips.

In their house Authakkutti and his mother talked about the jack tree and its lost fruits. The mother said, 'If only we knew to whom the land belonged!'

Authakkutti said, 'Whoever that may be, no one would use it.' He continued after a pause, 'Nobody sowed the seed; no one watered it and no one nurtured it. It came on its own. They say it foretells evil fate.'

The mother said anxiously, 'Son, we don't want it. Let us stay away from it. What people say might be true, otherwise why has the tree came up on that spot itself?'

'Okay mother, we don't want it.'

The next day Authakkutti was digging some part of his land. Raman was busy working on his land.

'Authakkutti!'

The call was heard. Not knowing who called, Authakkutti stopped his work and looked around. He saw Raman looking at him. Authakkutti never expected Raman to call him, but Raman was the only one standing there looking at him.

Raman Nair said, in a trembling voice, 'I'm the one who called you, Authakkutti.'

Authakkutti stood listening but did not say a word. Raman Nair continued: 'These jackfruits are being wasted.'

Authakkutti's mother came out of the house and heard what Raman said. Authakkutti wanted to say something in response, but found it difficult to speak. Raman Nair asked – 'Why don't we get the land measured to ascertain the boundary?'

Authakkutti said – 'Yes, we shall.'

Raman Nair entered into details – 'We shall share the expenses.'

Authakkutti replied, 'I'm prepared to meet my share of the expenses.'

Both the houses experienced a sense of inexpressible relief that day. Authakkutti felt that Raman's suggestion was a good solution to the problem. He asked his mother – 'Couldn't they have done it *then*, mother?'

The mother spoke in an undertone – 'I had suggested it to your father. He said there was no need of doing it and then he went to quarrel with them.'

Authakkutti asked in surprise – 'Was it he who started the quarrel?'

She said in more of an undertone, 'Of course it was he. He went deliberately to quarrel. That man was cutting some twigs; your father went to him and prevented him from cutting twigs. That man had the knife in hand. That was how it all came about.' She added, after a while of thought, 'We lost our lord of the house and they lost theirs.'

In Raman Nair's house also there was the same talk. Pappu Nair too had been stubborn in his decision not to measure the land. Raman's mother described the calamity in undertones and said that Chacko was the one who started the quarrel. She concluded with a deep sigh: 'We lost our lord of the house and they lost theirs.'

The great fear that ravaged their hearts for a long time disappeared and the two women slept peacefully that night. The next day Raman and Authakkutti met each other on the road. They did not turn back. Each wanted to ask the other the formal question of where he had been. The query came to the tip of their tongues but remained unuttered. After passing each other and walking five or eight feet, both of them turned round to face the other.

Authakkutti asked, 'When shall we get the land measured? You see, those jackfruits are getting ripe.'

Raman Nair suggested, 'Why not tomorrow? If the fruits are ripe, we shall gather them today and divide them equally between ourselves.'

Authakkutti told him, 'There are snakes in that forest.'

'Yes, huge cobras! We shall clear the forest first.'

That evening Authakkutti and Raman Nair cleared the forest and killed three or four snakes. Next day Authakkutti climbed up the jack tree. Raman stood below watching him, with the two mothers by his side. It was years since the two women had stood together.

Raman found a person who knew how to measure the land, but he demanded twenty rupees as his fee. When Raman told him this, Authakkutti asked – 'Should we waste money, Raman Nair?' Why don't we divide the land into two halves and separate them with a rope?'

Before he finished the question, Raman Nair said, 'Alright, I agree to that.'

Thus the boundary dispute ended. One jack tree and the banyan tree went to Authakkutti's share and Raman Nair got the other jack tree.

Now we can see the two women sitting next to each other and talking.

Translated by
B. Chandrika

The Farmer

That fifty-para paddy field is owned by someone in Vaikom. Kesavan Nair has been cultivating it for the last forty years. Before that, Kesavan Nair's uncle was its cultivator.

The lease-rent was minimal in the early days. Now it has increased slightly. During the month of Meenam every year, the paddy which is set apart as the lease-rent, is dried, filled in gunny bags and transported to Vaikom and handed over to the landlord. For the last so many years, this has been the practice. The ownership and possession rights of the fields lying on the four sides of this fifty-para land, has changed many hands during this period. But the landlord, and the cultivator of the fifty-para remain the same persons. For the landlord, all the paddy he gets is from this piece of land. The lessee is a traditional farmer. He too has only this piece of land in his possession.

Some ten years ago, when paddy prices were as high as five to seven rupees a bushel, rich people from Changanassery and Thiruvalla, had come there for paddy cultivation. They got on lease, extensive poddlers or groups of paddy fields. They used a tractor for deep-ploughing and new fertilizers, to produce bumper crops. And they made huge profits. And the style of paddy cultivation nowadays is just this. Kesavan Nair's fifty para is in the centre of a poddler cultivated by an industrialist.

That big-time farmer, Outhakkutty, met Kesavan Nair one day, on the mud-bund of the field. The crop in the 'fifty' is poor when compared to those around it. Outhakkutty broke in, by way of exchanging civilities: 'Why is the paddy not lush and robust enough? Didn't you use fertilizers?'

That question struck Kesavan Nair's heart.

The neighbouring farmer insinuates that the paddy he cultivates is inferior in growth!

'After you big guys came, can we drain out the water at the right times? No time is convenient enough for you. We can do farm work only at your convenience.'

Outhakkutty, an arch diplomat, said; 'Why do you say that, Uncle Kesavan? I had specifically arranged with my people to pay heed to your convenience.'

Kesavan Nair was cross. 'Oh! Nice arrangement indeed! I could wet the land only after my paddy seedlings had wilted in the sun. I went behind your servant, begging. He said he can't because you had instructed him not to give water to me. It's puncha-kandam and is true to its traditions, mind you.'

Outhakkutty had to counter that accusation. 'Will there be any such difficulty, if you do the sowing at the same time as in the neighbouring fields?'

Kesavan Nair was piqued. 'Don't teach me all that. It's not yesterday that I started cultivating paddy.'

Kesavan Nair continued, increasingly irritated, 'No one becomes a farmer by pouring in money, dumping fertilizers and raising a crop of paddy.'

Outhakkutty knew that Kesavan Nair aimed that dig at him. 'Why are you being cross, Uncle Kesavan?'

'I am not being cross. I was just mentioning some facts.'

After a few days, Kesavan Nair and Outhakkutty's servant quarrelled with each other, upon the mud-bund of the field. On all sides there was water. But the 'fifty' was parched dry and cracked up and the tillers were wilted. Kesavan Nair, heart broken at the sight, cut a breach in the mud-bund. The servant sealed it up. They pushed and jostled each other. It would have culminated in murder. Luckily, that did not happen. Three or four days later, the crop in Kesavan Nair's 'fifty' was submerged up to the tips of the plants in water. The top of the tillers were not at all to be seen above the water's surface. That servant's doing! When the time came for the sunning of Outhakkutty's paddy plants, the water was diverted to Kesavan Nair's 'fifty'. How is he to drain that water away? Where will he take it to? Can he drink it all up? Kesavan Nair's tillers began to rot.

Everyone said that it was indeed a high-handed action. But what is the use? Kesavan Nair went about looking for Othakkutty three or four days. He could not find him. Kesavan Nair didn't know what to do. That crop was doomed if the water remained like that for two more days. Kesavan Nair was like a mad man.

Kuttichovan, a friend of Kesavan Nair, asked in consternation, 'Why don't we cut open breaches on the bunds at night and divert the water back to the other fields?'

Kesavan Nair did not like that idea. He said, 'That should not be done in puncha-kandam. Cut open bunds in the dead of night! Can a farmer do that, Kutty? Let me perish. Even then, I will not do what should not be done.'

Then another friend, Kutty Mappila, said, 'Are all the things happening now, befitting a puncha-kandam? Well, well. Have you ever heard, not only in these fields, but anywhere in the land, something like denying water to the field surrounded by other fields, and flooding it with all the water, when not required?'

Kesavan Nair said in irrepressible anger and rage. 'Is he a farmer? Does he know the dharma of a farmer? He produces paddy crops, pumping in money. And makes money selling it. Does it make a farmer?'

Kuttichovan saw a gap in the argument and pressed home his argument. 'That's why I say, you should drain away the water from your field, cutting open the mud-bund at night. They don't care for any values. Why can't we follow suit?'

Kesavan Nair said he would never perpetrate that adharma. Kutty Mappila, who was listening to it all, said, half-soliloquising. 'So it was well and good that I leased out my piece of land to

Outhakkutty. Or else, my fate too would have been the same now.' Kuttichovan also said the same thing. Of that 500 acre poddler-complex, only Kesavan Nair's 5 acres remained outside Outhakutty's domain. The rest was in his possession. There was none to help Kesavan Nair, as a farmer. And everyone was sympathetic towards him. Listening to the talk of his friends, Kesavan Nair said, 'I too would have entrusted mine to him. But, what else is there for my livelihood? What work will I do? You, kutty Mappila, get at least 500 coconuts. Kuttychovan has four sons, working. I have only this field on lease. And I can eke out a living, only by tilling it.'

That was true. No one said anything. Kesavan Nair continued, 'From my ancestors' times we have been toiling on this piece of land.'

That night, the water in the 'fifty' somehow drained away. Someone had breached the mud-bunds at night. Certainly it was not Kesavan Nair. Since that water spread evenly into the fields surrounding that field, no ill effects had occurred to the crops of those fields. It was clear that the farmer of the neighbouring fields had let in water to that 'fifty' on purpose.

Next morning, Kesavan Nair went out to the field and saw for himself. He was flabbergasted. It was not relief that he felt at the crop being saved by the draining away of the water. Who had perpetrated this adharma? The weight of that sin would fall on him only! He had not known anything about it. He wondered how he was going to prove his innocence, if someone asked him about it. The infamy of opening a breach into a puncha-kandam would always trail him.

The poor man didn't look into the other fields to see if anything ill had happened to the crop in those fields. On the one hand, his fear of a scandal. On the other, his relief at his crop having escaped destruction. So, he returned home. He was afraid that, that day someone would turn up and ask him about it. So he shut himself up in a room and remained there in hiding, after arranging with his family to tell anyone who asked for him, that he was not there. Kutty Mappila and Kuttychovan came. He was too scared to meet even them.

Two days passed thus. On the third day, in the morning, before anyone woke up, Kesavan Nair went to the field and looked around. The weak tillers which had been flattened to the ground, had started rising up, in the sun's warmth. His crop wouldn't perish. After three or four days of getting the sun, the tillers should be soaked a little by letting in water for one day, and some manure put in. Then, the crop would be excellent, first rate. Everything pointed towards that possibility. The farmer's next thought was how to raise money to buy manure. He had to repay the debt of eighty bushels of paddy and 120 rupees including the seed-paddy and labour charges incurred for the present crop. The expenses for draining the water, besides. It would have been enough if he could get a hundred rupees more. The growth of the crop would be retarded if at least a smattering of manure was not put in. Where could he raise the money from? Who would give him money? The household expenses were met by the proceeds from the four milch cows. Kesavan Nair toyed with the idea of selling one of them to raise the funds. But his wife wouldn't agree to it. It was she who had raised the cows.

Kesavan Nair was standing lost in thought. His head was full of thoughts about the manure problem. He knew nothing else.

'The tillers are properly sunned, aren't they, Uncle Kesavan?'

Kesavan Nair turned around. It was Outhakutty. Suddenly Kesavan Nair's obsession about the adharma upset him. The adharma of cutting a breach at night in the mud-bund of a puncha-kandam. Wasn't it that adharma pursuing him? Outhakutty stood there as if he had caught the culprit. He, Kesavan Nair, should give him a proper explanation. He had to establish his innocence in the matter. With a troubled smile,

Kesavan Nair said, 'Upon my grand-uncle! Upon this punchakandam which is true to its tradition, it is not I who breached the bund, Outhakutty! I am a true farmer. A farmer worth his name would never do such an adharma.'

Outhakutty watched Kesavan Nair's anxiety. 'Why do you swear by your ancestors, Uncle Kesavan? It is not you who breached the bund. It's I who did it. I did it because I saw your paddy submerged, as I was coming along this way.'

Kesavan Nair was relieved. His eyes shone. 'Is it true? Tell me the truth! Oh, it's such a relief! May you do well in life, my boy! I feared I would have to carry the weight of this infamy with me till my death.'

Outhakutty once more said emphatically. 'Yes, Uncle Kesavan. It's I who did it. Although you hate me, can I hate you? When I saw that sight, my heart nearly stopped. I opened the breach. Let my paddy perish, if it has to, I said to myself.'

Kesavan Nair was not sorry about the crop being lost. That infamy!

Outhakkutty said, glancing all over the 'fifty'. 'If you could sprinkle a little manure, the crop would be excellent, Uncle Kesavan.'

'I was thinking of that just now.'

'Then you have to do it.'

'One should have money for that. Money! I don't have money.'

'If you want a good crop, you should spend money.'

'The times are such.'

Outhakkutty said, as if because of his fondness for Kesavan Nair: 'Uncle Kesavan! May I say something?'

Kesavan Nair raised his head and looked at Outhakkutty's face.

'Why are you taking all this trouble, Uncle Kesavan? I'll give you the lease-rent for the landlord at Vaikom and fifty bushels of paddy extra. Hand over the field to me. Why toil so much in your old age?'

Kesavan Nair suddenly became another person altogether. He was furious. Yet, controlling his anger, he said: 'No, no. Keep that thought to yourself Outhakkutty. We have cultivated this field right from the times of our ancestors. No one else shall cultivate it.'

'That's all right. You are the lessee of the Vaikom-landlord. And I am your lessee.'

'No. That won't do. I was born a farmer. Farming is my occupation. And I have five heads of cattle besides. They need the hay. No. It won't work, Outhakkutty...'

Kesavan Nair walked on without saying anything more. He was afraid that he might quarrel with Outhakkutty, if he stayed on and talked. Or, he would have to agree to what Outhakkutty proposed.

Outhakkutty couldn't help laughing, looking at that old man hurrying away.

No manure was put in the 'fifty'. The crop was bad. Dismal, that is. During the harvest season, Kesavan Nair could not get hold of reapers. All around, Outhakkutty's first-rate crop was there; if they reaped it, they would get two bushels of paddy as percentage wage. Would they reap that or Kesavan Nair's poor crop for which they wouldn't get even one-fourth that. Kesavan Nair went around requesting reapers to harvest his crop, for four or five days. The paddy was getting overripe. At last, the members of Kutty Mappila's and Kuttichovan's families, the servant Pulayan and his Pulayi and Kesavan Nair's family members together reaped the field. They couldn't even cut the hay. For that matter, there was not much hay there in the field.

The crop was very, very bad. It was doubtful whether there would be sufficient paddy to pay the lease-rent. Kutty Mappila, Kuttichovan and Kesavan Nair conferred together. Kutty Mappila's opinion was that the lease-rent need only be proportionate to the crop output. Till that moment, there wasn't even a grain of paddy as outstanding payment of rent. 'You can give more, if next year's crop is better.'

Kesavan Nair couldn't agree to that.

'This is the only piece of land the landlord has. And he has only this much of paddy to get. We have collected the crop. We should give the whole rent. The land will turn barren, if the landlord's tears fall on it.'

Kuttichovan asked, 'What if the entire crop is not sufficient to pay the rent?'

Kesavan Nair came up with a sudden answer: 'The deficit will be made good by buying some paddy.'

That evening, the boat was ready to carry the paddy to Vaikom. The whole of the paddy was kept on the threshing floor, after winnowing. The paddy set apart as lease-rent was measured, filled in gunny bags and carried to the waiting boat.

The entire crop was just sufficient for the payment of the lease-rent. What remained for Kesavan Nair was just a ton and a half bushels of paddy, spillage on the threshing floor and the chaff! He couldn't make good even the seed-paddy and the labour charges!

The lease-rent paddy was carried to the landlord's house. The landlord was a Thirumulpad. Kesavan Nair had sensed that there was a slight change of expression on Thirumulpad's face. What was unusual was that he asked whether the entire lease-rent paddy had been brought. And he made this comment: 'My information was that this year I would not get the entire lease-rent paddy.'

Kesavan Nair gave a hot repartee. 'Isn't it at least a hundred years, since we took this "fifty" for cultivation, Thirumeni? Is there even a grain of paddy outstanding as lease-rent payment till now?'

Thirumulpad didn't say a word.

The lease-rent paddy was measured out without leaving even a grain as deficit. Still, Thirumulpad's face didn't exhibit any trace of satisfaction.

He gave lunch to Kesavan Nair and the boatmen as usual. When Kesavan Nair approached, after lunch, to take his leave, Thirumulpad told him that he had something to say to him.

'What is it?' asked Kesavan Nair.

The reply was abrupt.

'Someone has approached me with an offer to take the land on an increased rate of rent. He is a very smart person too. Kesavassar, you should relinquish the land.'

Kesavan Nair stood there as if thunderstruck. He couldn't utter a word.

A few moments passed. Thirumulpad continued: 'First rate paddy field. You are enjoying it for a low rent. That's not possible now onwards. Leave the land free.'

Kesavan Nair came out of his daze: 'The land is yours. But, there are certain things we all should remember.'

'There is nothing to remember.'

An idea dawned upon Kesavan Nair. 'What increase of rent is proposed now?'

'A hundred bushels of paddy. And the party is very sound. How will I recover any arrears you may accumulate?'

Kesavan Nair argued hotly: 'So far there're no arrears.'

No one spoke for sometime. Kesavan Nair continued. 'Thirumeni, I shall give you that increased rate of rent.'

Yet, Thirumulpad was not satisfied. Kesavan Nair asked, 'Why don't you say something?'

'It's not good to entrust the land to weak parties henceforth.'

Kesavan Nair was angry. 'How do you know that I am weak? Did I ever cause any arrears?'

No answer.

Kesavan Nair continued: 'I'll tell you one thing, Thirumeni. I know who has approached you. It's Outhakkutty. But he is not a true farmer, Thirumeni. The likes of him don't love the soil. They'll put a lot of fertilizers, prodigally extract the fertility of the soil and raise good crops. After four or five years, your land will turn into useless, bran-like soil. Not even grass will sprout there.'

Thirumulpad was walking back and forth the length of the veranda. He didn't speak a word. Kesavan Nair continued to speak. The words choked his throat. His eyes brimmed with tears. 'It's this field I saw, when I was born. The sweat of my ancestors has also added to its fertility. I have loved only that field in my entire life.'

Kesavan Nair broke down. 'N-no! You shouldn't evict me from there, Thirumeni.'

Even Thirumulpad's heart seemed to melt a little. He said, 'I must get my rent.'

Kesavan Nair sobbed. In between, he said, 'I'll give you that rent.'

Kesavan Nair returned, having taken the same field for an increased rate of rent.

Usually, the field would be ploughed two to three times, while the soil was still dry, just after the harvest. The wages for it would be given as paddy right from the threshing floor. This year, there wasn't even a grain of paddy left after the harvest. The money borrowed for carrying out the framework of the last crop too had not been repaid. There was nowhere to borrow from either.

The next day after his return, Kesavan Nair called the ploughman and had the field ploughed once. He didn't even think of how he was going to pay them wages. From that day, the ploughmen pestered him for payment of wages. How could he have the land ploughed again, without paying the wages for the first ploughing?

Thus the field fell fallow. The neighbouring fields were regularly ploughed every month. The 'fifty' was overgrown with weeds.

Outhakkutty approached him still. He said he would give the increased rates of rent Kesavan Nair agreed to pay to the Vaikom landlord, plus fifty bushels of paddy. Kesavan Nair was enraged. 'No! Don't ever imagine that'll happen! I won't hand over this field to you.'

It was time for the sowing of the next crop. The work of putting up the mud-bunds was over. The water was being drained. The 'fifty' was lying vacant, without being ploughed, without weeding, without the soil being prepared. Poor Kesavan Nair didn't even have the necessary seed-paddy.

His fight then turned towards his wife. One cow must be sold. She didn't like the idea, though.

She said, 'We are pulling on, just on account of that cow. I won't agree.'

Kesavan Nair was incensed. 'How'll we sow the paddy, then?'

'Don't sow.'

'I am a farmer. I must sow.'

'Ah! A farmer, indeed!'

Kesavan Nair sold a cow without the consent of his wife. Even as the person who bought the cow went away tugging it along, she cursed: 'Damn this crop.'

The money the cow's sale brought in was sufficient only for ten bushels of seed-paddy and ten rupees for the labour charges.

Kesavan Nair tied up the seed-paddy and put it in water. He took out the seed the following day. Not even half of it had germinated. And he was supposed to sow that day itself. Kutty Mappila advised him to sow it as it was. It will germinate, lying in the soil! That's the only way out, besides. He did just that.

The paddy was growing robustly in the neighbouring fields. In the 'fifty', weeds had grown thickly. Not even a single tiller was to be seen. Kesavan Nair had the infamy of having spoiled the field.

The harvest that year was over. There was no need to reap the 'fifty'. The date of handing over the lease-rent paddy had expired. Thirumulpad reached the spot. Kesavan Nair was in hiding. For three days, Thirumulpad went about looking for him. He was not to be found.

The next day, Outhakkutty's men got into the 'fifty' and ploughed the field. Thirumulpad was standing on the mud-bund, looking on.

The sowing of the next crop was over. Early every morning, Kesavan Nair would go out to the fields, like a farmer who had a crop to look after. One watching him go would think that he really had a crop somewhere. He'd return only after the day had progressed. It was the habit of forty-odd years.

The paddy in the next 'fifty' was leaping as if challenging Kesavan Nair. He'd go there everyday. When once he spotted a slight yellowing of the plants, his heart burned. He sought out Outhakkutty and reported the matter. Not only that; he stood by and had the necessary remedial measures carried out.

Translated by
A.J. Thomas

The Story of Kettuthali

When a husband dies the wife might ask, 'Are you leaving me behind?' The mother asks the same question when her child dies; so does the husband when his wife breathes her last. In fact, everyone asks this question when someone dear to him or her dies.

But the question the wife poses when her husband leaves this world is quite significant. It is not like the mother's question, nor is it like that of a brother or a friend. Not at all like the question posed by the husband. True, death creates a void in their lives. The mother's sorrow is incomparably immense: she gave birth to the child, and brought him up with fond care and love. Her solid contribution to life. And she lost it. Her agony has a lot to do with something in her, something that ensures the continuity of the race. The brother thinks: we are so many, and we have lost one of us. And the husband misses his wife's love, care and all…

What about the wife?

That's different. What is the difference? Something to remember, to dilate upon. One can understand its significance when one remembers the man-woman relationship, family relationship – not only as a part of the economic set-up, but against the social backdrop of the history and metamorphosis of life over the years. Or it is enough to think of the kettuthali, the gold pendant strung on the bridal thread or chain, tied around her neck by the bridegroom at the wedding.

Have you not seen it nestling against the woman's throat, throbbing in the presence of life – her breathing in and out. Now, I suppose, you have understood the meaning of the wife's question: 'Have you deserted me?'

Yes, she asked: 'Are you deserting me?' And his mouth was still open as if he wanted to tell her something more. And his eyes were still half open – as if looking at her. But the eyes appeared to have a mica covering... He lay there as stiff as a log.

She expected an answer to her question. Yes, certainly he would say, 'Not at all.' He seemed to be gazing at his weeping wife. Again, she asked: 'Ah, no breath?'

And she discovered the hidden truth. She shook him, separated his eyelids a little more, pulled at his lips. And she fell on the dead body...

She could not believe what had happened. She disbelieved death. The reason was that her husband had loved her so much. And he lay there, in front of her, his hands and legs stretched, and in a comfortable position. Would he refuse to say something, having heard her weeping? Yes, she might have been reconciled to the bitter truth if he lay there, head severed. Even then, she might have tried to join the severed head with the trunk of his body.

She placed his head in her lap, and repeated her question. And the rude reality dawned on her: he was dead.

'Who's there now for me?'

The next question:

'Tell me... tell me...'

'What am I to do?'

There was no answer.

Again she tried to wrest an answer from him.

'What will I do?'

No answer.

She touched his eyelashes and lips, and insisted on an answer.

No answer came. She seemed to think that he would utter at least a word in reply even though he was dead.

Then followed the usual plaintive recounting of their mutual love! How he had scolded her for not having her dinner waiting for his return late at night.

The women of the neighbouring houses flocked around her and said something to console her. But she persisted with her loud question: 'Who's there for me? What will I do?'

Why? The departed soul might be close by grieving over her sorrow. And it might give her an answer.

The women around her answered the question. They could understand to some extent its meaning. To the question 'Who's there for me?' they might answer back, 'Can man live till the end of earth?' And they might conclude by saying, 'God's there for all.' To the question 'What will I do?' they might answer, 'God who made the mouth would also give something to eat.'

Even then, how long could one go on asking questions that remained unanswered?

And that day she was the talk of the neighbouring houses. A little girl! She got a husband when she was quite young. He loved her and she loved him, intensely. Husbands and wives do quarrel with each other. But in their home there was always the warmth of love and happiness. The neighbours spoke at great length about the happy life of the two 'youngsters'. They used to eat from the same plate. And occasionally he used to carry her on his waist – she would then be abashed. Once he drew a moustache on her face. Stories of this kind abounded. And all of them quite grasped the meaning and depth of the question, 'Are you deserting me?' Who was there to love her, to look after her? What would she do? Neither he nor she appeared to have any relatives. No one had turned up so far. None came when he was bedridden or when he died. But one thing was certain: there was a marriage. And that was indicated by the kettuthali, the bridal pendant on a string around her neck.

In all the houses nearby the question came up: how would she live? None could provide an answer. They lived on his earnings from the odd works he had done in the town – chopping wood, thatching roofs, and so on. How would she live now? The only possible answer was, she might live on somehow. One woman alone raised the pointed question. 'Supposing the destitute girl was not at all married? She would continue to live as she had lived in the past. Just take it that the marriage did not take place at all!'

That is true. Then what about the kettuthali? Does it not mean anything? Even if the old chain is removed the kettuthali would remain there. Even if a new husband comes, her kettuthali will not lose its place or significance. That is the significance the kettuthali has attained over the ages…

Throughout the day of his death, all the neighbouring women were near her. Each one of them said to her words of solace and comfort. The next day just a few called on her. Could they sit around her all the time? Three or four women together made her take a bath and drink a little rice gruel. Initially she was reluctant to drink. 'The dead are gone, will they come back to life if we starve?' They tried to put some sense into her head. They wiped her tears, and shed tears themselves. With the rice gruel in front, she burst into tears. They too joined her. And she muttered: 'Now I must drink it alone, all alone!'

The other women did not have to face such a pitiable reality. They had seen how happily she and her husband had lived. And now he had left her behind. She was all alone. An old lady wept bitterly holding her in her embrace and murmuring: 'Oh, my dear!'

The liquid food did not go down her dry throat.

Days passed. She was alone in the house. Her eyes dried up, having wept on and on, turning over in her mind the past bliss in the company of her husband. No tears welled up now:

merely a dull pain persisted in her eyes. 'And now what?' She was confronted with that question, quite weighty and painful. 'I've to live,' she told herself. Before the kettuthali was tied around her neck, the question had come up. A virgin can have expectations: one man would come to her one day, and she would have the occupation of being his wife. Expectations of this kind. And she had now been deprived of that occupation. Today, she had no hopes. Moreover, what did the grandmothers teach her? The kettuthali meant that she had become one man's property.

How to go on now? To wait for another man! That was something she could not even think of. Now that she had served a man – it was a veritable fulfillment of her life. It was not at all possible to have again the same sense of fulfillment. She felt the presence of the kettuthali around her neck: her God had vanished after tying it.

Tears again welled up in her eyes – the eyes, she thought, that had dried up long ago.

He had fondled her, caressed her, loved her. And she had became proud of being the object of such deep love and affection. She had been so dear to him. Naturally, she had become obstinate, had behaved like a child, like a passionate flirt, and affected innocence. A soul, sad and longing, hovered there, looking steadily at her, sorrowing and weeping. She felt its presence near her, as if it went round and round her. Its sobs touched her body. She felt a very hot kiss on her cheeks – a hot kiss wet with hot tears.

'What am I to do?' She asked.

The answer to the question was in the air – it was not expressed in words, it was not expressed at all. In the mild breeze, in the fluttering of leaves, in the chirping of birds, in the consoling words of the people? It was present.

'To be the wife of another man… no… I can't…' she said as if she heard the suggestion: 'Be the wife of another man!' She just could not restrain herself.

The zest to live: a woman can have only one occupation, to be the wife of a man. And this idea might have prompted her to say it aloud. The wonderful world through its mild wind, the melody of birds, and lovely and loving human beings beckoned her to live. There was only one way to do it: become the wife of another man. The helpless girl said to herself: 'To serve another man… No… it's not possible. The man may not like it. I don't know. I may even get beaten up…'

The kettuthali seemed to throb in her neck's small hollow. Again, the zest for life surged up within her. After all, she was still a young girl. She had not had enough of life.

She had learned what a husband may look for in a wife. She had to get the permission of the departed soul to become the wife of another man.

How to get that permission?

The dead man would not be able to see her suffer in life.

He always wanted her to be happy. Then how could he object if she sought happiness?

The dead body may not even have decomposed as yet. The neighbours, who had to struggle daily to earn a living, could not keep her company all the time. How could they who found it impossible to make both ends meet, give her food every day? As a result, she went one full day without any food. But she did not feel the hunger much.

But how many days could one starve? The next day she thought: how long will I have to live thus? Till death! When will that day come?

All her thoughts boiled down to a bowl of gruel. Parched throat, burning stomach. Where could she get the gruel from? How could she ask the neighbours? They have brought me something all these days, she thought. If I ask them, they might give me food today also. But what about tomorrow? She thought along these lines.

In that coolie's house there was nothing valuable to be sold. And no one came to her mind from whom she could seek some help.

It was a moment when one tries to find a way out. Not long-term planning. Just a bowl of gruel.

She was still optimistic. How else could she breathe?

Her eyes were roving…

A man was seen walking along the road. She tried to find out who he was. She looked steadily at him because he appeared to be someone known to her. Yes, he had come to her house along with her husband many a time. They were friends. Where was he now going?

Many details concerning the man flooded her memory. She did not know why and how. The details she already knew. He had not been married. He was a good worker, one who earned fat amounts in wages. They had always envied him. Her husband used to borrow money from him.

He came straight to the house. And she stood up.

He lingered a while in front of the house, remaining silent.

He did not know what to say. He appeared to be a little upset. She too did not say anything.

She was shedding tears – an uninterrupted flow of tears down her cheeks. Perhaps she recalled the days when the visitor had come to her house in the company of her husband.

All of a sudden she remembered her duty as a host. Wiping her face, she said: 'Please come in, and be seated.'

No sooner did he hear the invitation than he stepped in…

And they had a lot of things to talk about – her husband's illness, his death…

He was sad.

He referred to the happy days he had spent with his friend, her late husband.

And she said: 'I know it all… He often spoke to me about your mutual friendship.'

Their conversation went on for a long time…

And they began discussing the future.

He asked: 'What do you plan to do?'

She replied: 'I'll get on… somehow… I've to live…' He looked steadily at her, and asked:

'Haven't you had anything to eat?'

'I've eaten...'

'You look so tired... Tell me the truth...'

She did not say anything.

He took out a packet.

She said hurriedly: 'No. I'm not starving... I'm tired because of the depressing thoughts...'

Quite emotionally he pleaded: 'Accept this. Don't doubt my intentions. Here. It'll be a solace to my dead friend...'

He offered money; she did not accept it.

He continued to speak as if broken-hearted, 'Won't you accept this from your brother?'

She wept... and her hand came forward to accept it, of course without her knowledge....

A kerosene lamp flickered in the hut. They were talking. What were they discussing? It was getting late. Why didn't she tell him that talking far into the night was not proper? Or, what was there to talk about for so long?

All of a sudden the lamp went out, or it was put out. Who did it? For what? Who knows....

The conversation continued, though in hushed voices. She tried to evade, and he to win her over with promises.

'Oh, God, no... no...'

Her voice was heard. There was pitch darkness – darkness that could hide anything!

'The body has not yet decomposed... No. Please...'

That was the voice of a tired woman.

The kettuthali might have trembled in fear. But it could not be seen in the darkness.

Their conversation continued...

She knew that he was a bachelor, and a friend of her late husband.

He might have told her that her husband asked him to look after her in case he (the husband) died. He might have told her that he would have her as his wife. He might also have promised her that he would never desert her. And her husband would only be happy at the turn of events. It was not an insult to the kettuthali he might have assured her.

She too might have told him a lot of things. She loved one, and she could not love another. It was not possible for her to serve another man. And she would be a complete failure as the wife of another man.

The man might have countered all her arguments quite emotionally. That he had no grudge against her still loving her dead husband, that he too loved him, that he would love her even if she was not inclined to serve him.

The door of the hut was shut, leaving a sigh of sorrow. 'Oh, God!'

Once again there was movement in the hut. Smoke went up again from the hut. She bathed, wore white clothes. And she kept awake till midnight, with her kerosene lamp burning. She bought a new mat and pillow. She kept meals ready for one. Sometimes she went to sleep on an empty stomach.

This was not the case when she had her husband. He used to return home very early. And they used to eat together. She now learnt to wait, warding off sleep. She also learned to wait on an empty stomach. That was her responsibility.

The kettuthali throbbed on her throat reminding her of her story.

He often spoke of another man; and also about an important rich man. He mentioned sometimes, that they too helped him look after her. He spoke very highly of them.

One night he came with that 'friend' of his...

Again the hushed conversation between the husband and wife was heard from the other side of the hut. Broken-hearted, she wailed: 'Don't destroy me!' He might have ordered her to obey with all the might of a husband. To obey one's husband was what the kettuthali dictated. That meant she wore besides the kettuthali another chain of idealism. Could she defy that chain of idealism?

Even then she might have asked her deceased husband what she was to do. But the soul had already left the place, and it could not give her a reply then.

One who had learned the message of the bridal chain, she could not disobey the 'order'. That too might be part of serving one's husband.

The two men entered the room. And the call of the kettuthali made her also get in…

The rich man came again.

Thus times passed. He brought some others also, one by one. She obeyed him, like a machine.

One of those days she waited for him till the small hours of the morning and he did not turn up. He did not come the next day too. No, he did not turn up the next four days…. And then, one night there was a brawl in the house at night – someone beat up some others and someone was chased away…

He questioned her how somebody else had come there without his knowledge or permission…

By night she could be seen in the dark corners of the city. She had no house, no nest. By day, she was seen drifting along the streets. And yet she lived on…

A little later people saw her as a beggar with festering sores all over her body sitting at the crossroads. Even then, her kettuthali was there, nestling against a festering sore on her emaciated body.

And one morning she was seen lying dead at the road junction.

True, once a man lovingly fondled that body. The kettuthali is a token of that deep love and affection – a token indicating that woman can have only one vocation; to be the wife of a man.

Did she show disrespect to her kettuthali? Who knows. Decide for yourself.

Translated by
G.N. Panikkar

The Handbag

Her grandma and her little brother were waiting for her from ten o'clock. She had written that she would arrive in the afternoon. Her college had closed the previous day.

'There she comes,' her little brother ran out of the gate, shouting. The grandma saw her granddaughter coming at a distance. The little brother ran to her and walked hanging upon her arms. It was a fulfilling sight for Grandma. Her granddaughter had dressed herself up in a sari. She was studying in a college. Just a year for her graduation. Vilasini found her way into the old woman's bosom between her outstretched arms. They just stood like that for a second, with their faces merged into one another. The old woman's eyes were filled with tears of joy. Vilasini became a little babe, a playful tiny tot. Her little brother snatched this opportune moment and got hold of the handbag in her hand. He asked her: 'Isn't it for me, sister?'

He then tried to open it. Vilasini took it back and said, 'I shall open it. Don't force it.'

The grandma asked: 'What is in it, dear?'

Vilasini replied: 'You can put money in it, and also the pen. It is for all that, Grandma. Everybody in our college has a handbag.'

'Is it for me?' her brother asked again.

'I will bring you one next time.'

Grandma said: 'It looks like the palm-leaf bag of olden times.'

Everyone laughed. Vilasini opened the bag and showed it. There were her pen, a few pieces of paper, two rupees and some cloth pieces inside the bag.

Grandma also admitted that it was a useful utensil.

Grandma looked at Vilasini from head to toe. Great changes had come upon her within three months. She was just a small child earlier – a mischievous little girl. She used to open her mouth like an infant, laugh and weep. Her grandma had scolded her for her pranks. She had been worried as to when and how she would grow up. She didn't even know how to wear a dhoti properly. Now she wore a sari. She had grown up. She knew many things. She had become a woman and she was conscious of being a woman. Grandma often sat before her looking into her large eyes. Would she still laugh aloud as before? Would she fight with her little brother? Would she pull a long face and grumble? No. That is how one grows up.

Vilasini was always dressed in a sari or some other costume. She would not bathe in the pond. Even her grandma had no admission to the bathing shed while she bathed.

Once Grandma told her mother: 'Vilasini is no more a kid.'

'Eh, what of that, Mother?'

'Hasn't she come of age?'

'So what?'

'No, I was just saying, there is a suitable age for certain things. It should be conducted then.'

Then Vilasini came there. Her mother said, 'Oh! We needn't bother about it now. After all, she is only studying.'

Vilasini left the place quickly. Grandma continued: 'Let her continue studying. Can't one study even after marriage?'

'That is not possible, Mother.'

The old woman remarked after some time: 'If she is not married now, she will not be able to study.'

'Isn't it enough if she gets a good job, Mother?'

'Can a job be a substitute for marriage?'

Grandma used to talk about her like that quite frequently. Nobody else took her growing up seriously. Vilasini could not bear her grandma's gaze. Grandma was not just looking at her but at her youth. She would shrink under that piercing gaze. She would blush while talking to her grandmother. Grandma understood all that. Yet she felt closer to her grandma. She did not know why. It was perhaps because Grandma alone had understood what she wanted.

When alone, Vilasini was always thoughtful. She could not help looking at her rising breasts. She ran away from the sight of men. She scolded her little brother who went about without wearing a dhoti. Her shyness was gradually changing.

College was about to reopen. The day of her departure arrived. Grandma came into her room as she stood dressed up to go. She wanted to say something. The old woman's smile was meaningful. Vilasini asked her smiling: 'What is it, Grandma?'

Grandma looked straight into her eyes. She put her head down pretending to be looking at her dress. Grandma asked: 'How many people are there in the place where you are staying?'

'About sixty, Grandma.'

'Are the servants also women?'

Vilasini understood Grandma's line of thought. She felt upset for no reason. She murmured mechanically, 'Yes!' She went out of the room quickly. Grandma followed her. As she reached the gate, Grandma said: 'Take care of your body, dear.'

Vilasini walked away without saying anything in response. She understood that the old woman had read the goings-on in her mind. Grandma repeatedly reminded Vilasini's mother that the girl had come of age.

The lady asked, 'So what, Mother?' Grandma said, 'She is conscious of the fact that she has come of age. At a certain age, the grip on the mind gets lost. You have to be cautious then. She is after all staying alone.'

'She is more sensible than we are.'

Grandma did not feel convinced on that issue. She said, 'Whether sensible or not, a woman is always a woman.'

The days of anxiety for Grandma passed by.

Vilasini returned home during the next vacation. Her grandma and her little brother received her at the gate as usual. Grandma noticed in a moment the changes that had come upon her during the six months. She had put on a little more fat. Though she had worn more clothes, her breasts still looked conspicuous. Many pimples had ripened upon her blood-filled cheeks. Her voice had thickened. She was no more a girl, but a woman. Her eyes were still and unmoving. They seemed to have got stuck at some point. Generally speaking, her ways indicated that the opportune moment had passed. The fullness of growth… Isn't that the point at which the withering of the blossom begins?

Had she passed beyond the stage at which a woman develops a sense of curiosity? Had she experienced it already? That was what the Grandma suspected.

Her little brother caught hold of the handbag. She didn't give it. She scolded him. The Grandma found that the bag now bore a lock.

Vilasini liked solitude. She kept on sitting with a book open before her. Then the little brother would shout: 'Sister is not reading anything. She is just sitting idle with the book open before her.'

She used to hum some lines of a passionate love song. Her inner being merged into its melancholic rhythm. As she sat thus with her eyes closed, a deep sigh would fetch her back into the world of reality. There was a dream in her eyes. She used to open her handbag, take out some letters and read them. Then she would hold them close to her bosom. Lost in ecstatic dreams, her face would then stretch forward yearning for a kiss.

Grandma began to pester her mother with stronger words.

'I would like to see a child born to her before I die.' Her mother then replied: 'Isn't she studying?'

'Studying and studying, she will turn out to be an old dame. Then nobody will look at her.'

Grandma then approached Vilasini with her wish. She said: 'Nobody needs search for anyone for me.'

One day she wrote a letter and sent it through her little brother to be posted. The envelope emitted a fragrance as it had remained inside her bag. He smelt it all along the way. When he returned, he asked her: 'Who is this Vijayan, sister? What a name!'

Vilasini closed his mouth.

That vacation was at last over. As she was about to leave, her little brother said, 'Please give me that bag, when you come next time.'

Vilasini started studying abroad from that year onwards.

She was very brilliant in her studies. She received many prizes.

Once she sent a copy of her photograph along with her letter. Grandma looked at it with great curiosity. She had grown thinner. Though she had become very slim, she lacked her earlier loveliness. There was fatigue in her eyes. Grandma was inquisitive about the girl who was standing close to her in the photograph. Her mother replied: 'She is her close friend. Vilasini writes about her in all her letters. Don't you remember, Mother? They live in the same room.'

Grandma examined her face carefully. She is also as thin as Vilasini is. Grandma said: 'Men may sit and walk about with their hands on the shoulders of one another. But do women also do that? What kind of love is that?'

Vilasini's mother replied: 'That is the fashion now.'

'Fine fashion, indeed! They appear like husband and wife.'

'What of that, Mother?'

'I was just asking,' Grandma once again examined the photograph and said. 'The eyes of both of them look sunk.'

'Aren't they studying? It is tiring.'

'Both of them have handbags and they are bulging.'

'All girl students carry them.'

After this, Grandma used to repeat the question quite frequently: 'Is it enough if the girl studies all the time?'

'She will get a job.'

Grandma smiled meaningfully. She asked: 'Is marriage just for a living? Aren't you too a woman?' Grandma asked after some time: 'What if something untoward happens to the girl?'

Vilasini's mother firmly asserted that it would never happen to her daughter. Grandmother used to listen carefully to Vilasini's letters read out to her. She was not pleased with them, generally.

That was not the letter she was expected to write. Vilasini used to enquire after Grandma. But that was not enough. Grandma remarked complainingly: 'She is doing well. But she does not have much concern about us.'

She had more things to say: 'I only wish my child was married and had children. Women can love only if they have children. Vilasini loves only her friend who stays in her room. One can understand that from that pose.'

Four years passed. Vilasini was to come home during that vacation. Her letter had come. Grandma waited for her anxiously. She took part actively in all the preparations for her reception. She cleaned up the house. When a room was prepared according to her instructions, Grandma asked: 'What is this for? Can't she sleep with me like last time? What is the need for a separate room?'

How can such a question be answered?

The day arrived at last. Grandma was waiting from morning. A car came and stopped at the gate exactly at the time she had informed she would arrive. For a moment, Grandma did not recognize the person who came out of the car.

'What news, Grandma? Are you alright?' She asked her.

Grandma stood stunned. Vilasini walked towards her room without waiting for her response. Grandma also accompanied her. Grandma was baffled. Vilasini was wearing high-heeled slippers. Her dress was unfamiliar. Her hair was bobbed. Doesn't she oil her hair? Her face was pale. Or was it smeared with lime. Her eyes were lifeless. They were sunk deep. Grandma's eyes came down to her breast. There was not even a suggestion. Grandma's eyes were filled with tears. Was it the ghost of her granddaughter? She asked, sobbing: 'What has happened to you, child?'

'Eh? What is it, Grandma?'

'Why have you shrunk like this?'

'You go out and sit there, Grandma. I shall come to you. I shall tell you everything.'

Grandmother burst out crying. She could not bear it. Go out and sit there! That old woman walked away, trembling.

Vilasini's little brother came running to meet his sister. He also stood stunned at the door, seeing an unfamiliar figure in the room. She went up to him and, holding his chin with her two fingers, asked him: 'Why do you look so dirty?'

He did not say anything. He had come there thinking of many things. That he would embrace her, kiss her, snatch away her handbag. He had many such hopes. But he was stopped short as if at the touch of something very cold.

Vilasini said: 'Go and come back after you've had a bath.'

He too went out in silence. He fell on Grandma's lap and began to weep. The loving sister who excitedly went out with him after the butterfly and who cheerfully played with him was now lost to him. His heart had surged high, but had now become frozen.

When her mother reached there Vilasini had already bolted her room. Mother called her from outside: 'Daughter! Open the door! Let me see you!'

'I'm coming Mother! Excuse me for a while.'

Mother joined Grandma. She answered Grandma's complaints: 'Isn't she educated? We shouldn't find fault with her.'

An hour later, she came out well dressed. She wore a smile. It was as artificial as her dress.

She looked like a ghost of womanhood. The simplicity and tenderness of a feminine heart was missing. If she became a mother – no, she would not be a mother – that would be considered a burden. If at all such a thing happened, she would entrust the baby's upbringing to someone else. If the baby urinated, when she held it in her arms once in a while, she would drop it on the floor. She had nothing sacred to offer a man. That relationship would just be a contract. She might give him up one fine morning fifteen years later. But those lipstick-coated lips would still be smiling.

Vilasini was very formal and systematic in everything. She set up a time for everything. Days passed. She was not pleased with life there. One day Grandma told Vilasini's mother:

'Why is this girl so thin!'

'That's what I am also worried about.'

Grandma said after some thought:

'She looks like a woman after abortion.'

'Shh! Keep quiet! What a shame!'

'No, I was just saying.'

Her little brother who was hanging around her room came in running. He said, panting, 'Mother, Sister smokes cigarettes. She took one from that bag and lighted it.'

Grandma heaved a deep sigh.

Whenever she went out in the evening, she would come back only at nine in the night.

One day Grandmother asked her if that was proper. What did she talk about for so long with the cook! All that was wrong. But what could that poor old woman do? She observed all her movements carefully.

After a week, she left for Trivandrum. She was not so happy with the life at home.

One more week passed.

One day, Vilasini's little brother came running in with a handbag. He saw it lying on the road as he was coming from school. It was somebody's lost bag from the bus. Thus he got what he had been pining for. He gave it to his mother to open.

The woman was very reluctant to open it. But she was longing to know the contents of the bag held as a prop by fashionable society ladies. That desire had grown beyond control. Her daughter had such a bag. Grandma was also very inquisitive. They broke open the handbag.

For Grandma it was a novel phenomenon. She felt as though a new world had been opened up. These, then, belonged to fashionable ladies. Her granddaughter also had a similar handbag. She asked Vilasini's mother:

'To how many men, might Vilasini have written like this?'

'I don't know.'

Grandma spoke out with contempt: 'Who can't she flirt with? The cook, or any number of men? Why should she be afraid?'

The other woman did not say anything. Grandma continued: 'No wonder, she looks drained and dried up. Everyone of this type will go crazy.'

No one spoke for a while. Vilasini's mother was lost in thought. It took sometime for Vilasini's little brother to get back the bag from her.

Grandma continued: 'That umbrella with the new type of handle also suits these dames. How long have I been telling you that a girl should be wedded to a man at the right time?'

Translated by
Jancy James

The Best of

Thakazhi Sivasankara Pillai

Thakazhi is the recipient of many awards and honours, the more prestigious among them being the Bharatiya Jnanpith Award (1984), The Soviet Land Nehru Award (1974), The Sahitya Akademi Award (1957) and Vayalar Rama Varma Award (1980). The present book contains a selection of fourteen stories which reflect his many-faceted genius.

K.M. George was an eminent author and editor in Malayalam and English. His works have received various literary awards including the Bharatiya Bhasha Parishad Award and the Kerala government's Ezuthachan Puraskaram. He is the recipient of the Soviet Land Nehru Award, the Padma Shri and the fellowship of the Kerala Sahitya Akademi.